Blood Money

Penn Scripter

Troll River Publications

www.trollriverpub.com

Blood Money

Copyright ©2025 by Penn Scripter

ebook ISBN: 978-1-967090-03-7
Softcover ISBN: 978-1-967090-04-4

Book Cover by: Get Covers

Editor/s: Ravi Banthia

Join the fun with Author Penn Scripter for giveaways, updates, and new release opportunities at:

https://www.pennscripter.com/

Penn Scripter

Unexpected Paranormal Romance

DEDICATION

FOR MY BELOVED MOM, who has been my unwavering support and source of inspiration. Thank you for your everlasting belief in me. Your love and encouragement have shaped my journey. This book is a testament to your faith in my dreams. I am forever grateful.

Chapter 0

My mother named me Chamomile, after the taste of my blood.

Even though she'd never tasted the red liquid running through my veins, they had. It was tradition for a creature like me to be named for how my blood bloomed over those monster's tongues. That's what I was told, anyway. It must be true since they called my mother Pepper. Pepper Eirian.

I lived in a little cage under a big house filled with screams. Until the day before my twelfth birthday, it was all I'd known.

"Miles, get up." Mother shook me awake. She'd never called me Chamomile. Always Miles. I guessed because she didn't like what my full name represented.

My eyes snapped open. "It's not my day."

Once a week, they would bite my arms, my neck, and my legs. Tomorrow was my day for the demons to feed. For them to drain the blood from my veins. For me to die of a thousand needles embedded in my flesh.

"Do you trust me?" Mother reached for me and pulled away the green army blanket serving as a comforter.

I nodded. "Yes."

Her emancipated arms gathered me onto her chest, and I wrapped my spindly legs around her thin waist. The sheer, plain cream dress was my favorite because it had pockets. Pockets carried secrets. Secrets like candy, small toys, and even weapons like little knives.

Mother carried me past the door of my cage, and down the aisle of barred cells. Most the other rooms were empty. We passed by a moaning man, spread across his cot, recovering from the night before.

Fewer people than normal slept or recovered from the night before in their barred stalls. Even down in the cellar, I could hear the screeches over the music. The pleading and laughter. The smell. I didn't want to find out where it came from.

My mother rushed through the hall and came to an abrupt halt. A door creaked, and Mother's hands shook. I tried to look, but she pinned my chin to her shoulder so I couldn't turn around.

"Eli..." she said. "Let me through."

Eli Florentine. It took me long years of listening to snippets, but Eli was the head recruiter for regular blood slaves known as "drudges." If one of the enclave members requested a certain blood type, Eli brought in the body. Not a dead one, but the person he brought might as well be. Even though I knew he was bad news, Eli was also the only one who hadn't sunk his fangs into me.

Eli's calm voice chilled the room. "Let me take her."

"No!" Mother gripped me tighter and took a step back. She shuffled me to one arm, but I was too heavy for her to hold. I started sliding down her side.

Behind us, I saw a shadow, the outline of a man. I couldn't make out much except blond hair, a shushing finger over his mouth, and blue eyes pleading for me to stay quiet.

"Momma—" I said.

"Liebling—" Eli began at the same time as he stretched a hand with clawlike nails toward me.

Soon as my feet hit the ground. Mother jerked her hand and pulled out a silver pen.

"Wait!" Eli threw up his hands, blocking his face. "Pepper! Don't scare her!"

"How do you know what she's feeling?" My mother bared her teeth. Her shaking hand holding mine tightened, promising she wouldn't let me go. Her other hand aimed the pen level with his head.

"You're spiraling." He lowered his hands. "The others will know something's wrong." His eyes glittered. "I can take her and get her out safely."

I held my mother's waist and hid my face in her dress as I willed her to say no. I didn't want to go with the demon.

"You didn't answer my question." Mother seethed. "How dare you touch my child!"

"Pepper, I wouldn't—ahhh!" Eli threw up his hands as a beam of red light formed a dot over his fingers. Red light, thin as paper, split the darkness. Eli cursed and pushed his face to the wall, covering his left eye.

"Fine then, woman! I'll do what I can."

Mother ran with me in tow. We passed stairs, down the hallway. Down to a place I knew all too well.

They called it the medical bay. I called it hell. It held an empty counter, locked cabinets, and a table with straps to hold a "patient" down—for my safety, they said. I think they didn't want me flailing and scratching their eyes out.

"Mama?"

She whipped us around a corner, knelt to my level, and put a finger to her mouth.

Wide-eyed I nodded.

A gust of wind passed by, and Pepper peeked around the corner. She led us through the dark hall into the one room I hated most of all. The flat metal table, now a bed of nails, stood in the middle of it. Using their sharp canines, demons had ripped into me here until I went unconscious. It was not my favorite room.

Before I could complain, Pepper pulled out folding stairs and set them under the slit of a window. She climbed the steps and pushed the glass pane. It opened, and she took a stuttering breath. "Thank all, he did it."

An opening! We could escape!

She climbed down and knelt by my side. "Listen, Miles, you need to go now, okay?"

"But you're coming too?" My hands cupped my mother's face.

A great roar echoed off the walls, and thunder shook the house.

Mother wasted no time. She hauled me up the ladder and guided my head through the opening. The metal frame squeezed the sides of my face. It felt like getting a wind burn. My ears scraped against the window frame.

A door banged, and my mother's hands were ripped away.

"Let her leave!" Mother cried.

I couldn't turn to see even if I wanted to. My head remained pinned between the window frame. If they pulled me back, that might hurt. A lot.

I heard scuffling, and growls.

"Grab the child!" someone screeched. "The child!"

"No!" Eli roared. "It's too dangerous for her to stay."

With added effort, my head came free, but the rest of my body teetered inside. Someone shoved me through, the scraping of the window cutting into my chest, then my stomach, and finally my knees until I could claw the rest of the way through.

Long streaks of blood dripped from my head. My knees were scuffed, and the sharp metal in my shoulder ached where I'd squeezed through the window frame. The threadbare gown I wore, stained from grass and blood, felt paper thin against the cold autumn sky. Sunlight. A wash of white obliterated my sight.

"Momma..." I turned around and, in my illogical sense, made to pull my mom out of the hole that I had squeezed through. But I didn't have time to hurt, to tend my wounds, or to help my mother.

"Miles, run!" Mother cried.

I'd never forget the terror in my mother's eyes. Monsters swarmed, and as she reached for me, they engulfed her. Pepper was whisked away from sight and replaced by piercing blue eyes that scowled at me through the crack in the window.

"Do as she says, little morsel." An old dagger and a brown paper bag were tossed my way.

Fleeing wasn't hard. Ashamed, I took the package and scrambled away without my mother. I did what she said and ran.

CHAPTER 1

Nine years later...

A PAIR OF YELLOW EYES followed me as I walked from the dirt parking lot near the edge of festive university students. When I pulled in, desert partygoers were dancing, socializing and walking the grounds in full Gothic regalia. Everyone here craved being watched. I didn't. I'd only gone to the rave for information about my mother's whereabouts.

I pulled out my cell with a hot pink Hello Kitty phone case and started scrolling for messages.

"Scared?" Lilly, my friend and fellow college student, moved through the parked cars like a cat on the prowl. She wore jeans and a knitted white bikini top. Her red hair bounced with every footstep, and her sparkling blue eyes fixated on me.

"Of course not." I scoffed.

I had nothing to fear from humans claiming they were vampires, posing with fake teeth and drowning in black lace. Real monsters were out there, and none of these coeds hit the mark.

Unbeknownst to humans, vampires were only about five percent of the world's population. It was unlikely one of the undead roamed a college party. Yet, here I was, in fancy jeans and a white blouse, because Lilly found someone that could give me information about my mother. That and a few clients encouraged me to come.

Turns out there was a market for blood by these wannabe vampires, and they'd pay handsomely. It was enough money to pay for a room, college tuition, and necessities. It was also easy. Trying to look for my mother and holding down a job and school was too much even with hiring a PI, but I didn't donate solely for money.

Mostly, I wanted information. Any scrap of gossip that might let me find the one person who'd put my life before her own was worth a night of being bled. Mother, I will find you.

The celebration was an invite-only rave. Lucky me. My clients requested me, and Lilly organized this event so I could talk to one Diego Sanderson.

Everyone was tight-lipped about what went on during these events. Not that anyone was doing anything illegal out in plain sight. The more illicit goods and services were hidden out of sight in tents. Police might have an issue with my boot knife, but if anyone besides our inner circle knew what went down, it was likely the police would show up, and not only because of the contraband.

If my vanilla-mocha-drinking butt got put in the slammer... well, I'd heard women inmates were hard core. I shuddered, not at the company I might have behind bars, but because small cages reminded me too much of my past.

For the fifth time in twenty paces, my eyes traveled back to my faded-blue Honda sitting in a cleared field doubling as a dirt parking lot.

"You won't find any answers in your car." Lilly's topaz eyes sparkled in mischief. She had the bluest eyes I'd ever seen, and a body built for sin.

"Do you think this Diego will know anything?" I stood at the ragged edge of the last line of parked cars and glanced at the throng of people. A sea of black lace and topless guys in leather pants mingled in the center of a horseshoe ring of tents.

"He works for one of the echelon, so you want to ingratiate yourself." Lilly turned pouting with her hands on her hips. "I went to the trouble of making this appointment. Don't you have faith in me?"

Lilly knew enough about me and my mission to find the Florentine vampires. A house of real vampires. Not these college students that put in capped teeth, went to raves, and tried desperately to convince everyone around them they were children of the night.

Hopefully, this Diego would point me in the right direction.

My fervent wish was to find my mother and get her out of the hellhole she'd selflessly gotten me out of. I had to keep believing she was still alive.

I'd tried to find the Florentine vampires, but they moved frequently, and I had no way to track them down once Child Protective Services pulled me off the streets after my escape. I'd ceased being "Chamomile" and shortened my name to "Miles" to throw off the monsters. My twelve-year-old brain thought that would be enough to keep my past from finding me, but I needn't have worried.

No one searched for me after that night Mother helped me flee the Florentines.

This appointment was a long shot. I had to try. For my mother's sake.

"Lilly, I have faith in you. I just don't have much optimism for anyone else." I self-consciously pulled the delicate gauze scarf around my neck higher. The fuchsia accessory hid ugly scars. They were my calling card—both the scars and the scarf. New clients recognized me as the girl with color around her neck. That's how my contact would recognize me. Pink would stick out in a place smothered in black.

"Darling, I'm sure Diego can help you." Lilly pulled out a small perfume bottle and held it up. "Now stay still. This brand is all the rage." She sprayed two pumps under my chin and tucked the fragrance away.

Lilly had some major skills in the makeup department. If I ever needed a disguise to get out of town, she was the person I'd call.

From inside the edge of partygoers, the same pair of yellow catlike eyes dared me to enter the fray. The man attached to those yellow eyes was a gorgeous tall blond pretender wearing a blue suit. He was surrounded by a sea of black lace, Gothic motif, and people wearing a range of iris-color-enhancing contact lenses. He wasn't the only one wishing to be somebody else, something else. Anything else but human.

The monsters I'd dealt with did everything within their power to fit in. These people were doing anything to look like movie vampires, or what they thought demons looked like. If only they knew the reality.

Vampires look exactly like humans. The hair, the eyes, the skin. Most bloodsuckers are beautiful and employ various talents of seduction to lure their prey. What they have that people don't, what really gives them away, are a set of canine teeth that get exposed when they are ready to feed.

Dentists call it hyperdontia. The condition means that someone might have one or two extra teeth. Those are humans with extra calcium. Anyone that has a set of canines extending behind the flat human-sized ones are vampires.

Mr. Gorgeous Pretender smiled and flashed a pair of porcelain "sharpies" far longer than any humans. Implants? Dentures? Stick-ons maybe. They were out for show. Underneath the Lestat impression, this man possessed allure. Also, he wasn't wearing pure black—a clue he might be my contact.

"Dear Lord, is that Diego Sanderson?" I whispered over my shoulder to Lilly.

But she was gone. Nothing but wind caught my question.

Typical. She always left the fun part to me.

I took a deep breath and wandered to the edge of the fray. Let it be known that I, "Miles" Chamomile Makayla Evans Eirian, was not a flake. I held my end of the bargain. My word was my bond. If I broke a bargain with someone, that meant I was unreliable. If I became undependable to others, I became unreliable to myself. Then I wouldn't be good to anyone.

"What's your name?" Mr. Gorgeous spoke without a lisp that real people with removable teeth could not imitate without practice. Lots and lots of practice. He held an air of superiority in a blue suit that could make a girl swoon, but he loomed over me soon after I approached.

Mr. Gorgeous reminded me too much of the monsters that had drained my kind dry over and over. His vertically-slit yellow iris contacts were fake and disconcerting, and his needle-thin canines were in front and not hidden in the back, but he had the aura down flat.

He stared at me, waiting for an answer, bemusement curving his lips. I couldn't tell if his canines extended or if he thinned his bottom lip to make it look like they did. Still, panic struck me.

Catatonic helplessness rooted me to the spot. I tried shaking off the rising terror, assuring myself with the laser pointer in the pocket of my jeans, reasoning myself out of this spiral of fear, using all my experiences with real vampires to calm down.

He's not real. He's not real. He's not real. My instincts didn't believe a word I told myself.

Run. Run. Run.

His slit pupils didn't dilate. His teeth weren't doubled, but everything else he had right. The motions, the look, the insufferable confidence. Everything was too coincidental for him not to have at least seen an eternal damned.

Which was who I was looking for because only a vampire would know about other vampires. If I could find one bloodsucker, then I might be able to find my mom. But Mr. Gorgeous's near likeness threw me off and made me revert to an twelve-year-old child. Alone. Afraid. Running from monsters with nothing more than an antique blade. The heirloom was more than the size of a pocketknife but shorter than a throwing blade, and part of a life I'd left behind.

His smile faded, and a film of concern clouded his face. Then he blinked and wrapped his hand in mine. Mr. Gorgeous radiated heat.

"Hey," he said, his tone soft. "Are you all right?"

A true vampire could imitate life, but his human reaction made me feel better all the same. I broke out of my fright and started breathing again. "Fine. I'm fine."

He smiled with his sharp teeth once more in impish delight. "You seem new to the scene."

"And you seem to like scaring the crap out of people." I flashed an angry glare at him.

"Guilty." Mr. Gorgeous laughed, releasing my hand. "I do like watching people's reactions. But I like frightening beautiful young ladies the most." He gestured to himself. "Thomas."

A wave of relief let the last of my tension go. He wasn't the man I was supposed to meet. Not that I wouldn't go through with the deal if he were.

"Miles." I gestured to myself.

"Beautiful name for a beautiful lady."

Oh, a charmer. One never knew where a client would come from. "Thank you."

I started looking around. Diego, the person I'd made an appointment with, said he'd be wearing a suit. Which was why I thought Thomas was my contact.

"What brings you here, Miles?" Thomas, not Tom, purred my name.

Rule number one about vampires, fake or real, don't abbreviate their name. It's rude. They get offended. Real vampires are known for flying off the handle and starting fights that spill gore over everyone and everything for shortening their illustrious name.

"I'm meeting someone." Within the ocean of vampire Goths, I hoped Diego would wear something other than black.

"How much for an ounce?" He eyed my neck.

I faced him with a smile. "How do you know I'm not here to buy?"

He raised his hand and tickled the ends of my scarf. "You're not the only donor who wants to cover their marks."

"I already have an appointment." I winced and pulled away, wanting to find a mirror to see if my scars were showing. "I'm sorry, but another time?"

"So formal." Thomas smirked. His fangs pinched his lower lip.

From twenty feet away, a pair of glasses shimmered. Black eyes fixed on me. A dark-haired, olive-skinned kid in a black blazer and khakis came strolling over. His lopsided smile and shorter stature disarmed any panic button.

"Excuse me," I said, dismissing Thomas and stepped up to the new guy.

"Hello," New Guy said. "Are you Miles?" His gaze roamed over my fuchsia gauze scarf then glared over my shoulder as if he was mentally saying to Thomas, Back off.

"Yes," I said, aware of Mr. Gorgeous stepping up behind me. "Are you Diego Sanderson?"

The kid's attention refocused on me, and he nodded with that disarming grin. "That's me."

Oh, thank the Lord.

Diego was no taller than my own five-foot-nine height. Messy short black hair, nerd glasses that hid his dark eyes, and a face that screamed naïve—take advantage of me made a world of difference relieving my apprehension. Donating my blood to wannabe vampires paid the rent but made for nerve-wracking first meetings.

Behind me Thomas's buttery voice sent my spine rigid. "Sanderson."

Diego flicked his eyes over to Thomas, grinned, and nodded. "Hi, Tom."

Ouch.

In etiquette terms, Diego might as well have slapped Thomas in the face. Shortening a vampire's name, even a wannabe vampire, was like telling him his rank and title were worthless. I even knew of some humans that didn't like their names shortened.

"I was not done talking with the lady." Thomas snarled and stepped closer to my back, and dread sank all the way to my feet.

"She came here at my request." Diego extended his elbow, inviting me to slip my hand into the harbor of his arm.

Thomas's warm hand settled on my shoulder, and words whispered in my ear. "Don't go with him, Miles."

Diego remained smiling, but his eyes grew intense. He wasn't looking at me, but at Thomas.

The pause in conversation sent the tiny hairs along my neck to stand on end.

"Another time, Thomas," I said.

Thomas's hand slipped off my shoulder, and Diego broke out in a triumphant grin.

"Miles, let's talk away from prying eyes." Sanderson swept me away from the crowd and toward the parking lot.

I looked back to find Thomas ramrod straight, lips pressed thin with a look of pity in his eyes. "It was nice to meet you, Miles."

Damn. Why did I feel like I made the wrong call?

I wanted to get Thomas's contact info, but it didn't matter. He backed away and disappeared into the fray without a trace. Freaking Thomas had vampire mystic in spades.

Diego knew him, so maybe I could get Thomas's cell from him if Diego's intel didn't pan out.

I pulled myself together as Diego navigated us through the parked cars. He marched like a man on a mission, but I didn't let my guard down.

"Excuse me, Diego, that's far enough." I stopped and pulled him to a halt.

He turned and flashed wide eyes of worry but managed a pleasant grin. I was beginning to see how he used his innocent look to his own favor.

"This is as far as we go." I held out my palm.

Diego took my hand in both of his. Black doe eyes peered into my soul. "I understand. I know you have reservations, but we're almost there."

His puss-in-boots power of cute harmlessness nearly undid me. Voices in the back of my mind, soft but insistent, offered assurances. Diego won't hurt you. You can trust him. There's nothing to fear. Go with him. Gentle, invisible hands pulled me forward to a glowing white limo among the sedans and sports cars.

"Stop." I closed my eyes and pushed away those whispers in my head, giving a half-hearted attempt at pulling free from his hold.

Diego didn't release me. I knew I should be wary of him, but I couldn't pinpoint why.

His eyes widened as his lips parted and his face paled. "There is something different about you."

I tried tugging my hand free again, but he held it firm.

"Let me go."

With that he dropped his hold. "You don't want privacy?"

My head cleared, and I started going over my survival checklist. "I have a rule. No private places until I know you."

Diego searched my eyes. His sad imploring set off all my warning bells.

"Miles, I will not hurt you. I promise. You know my word is good, right?" His words settled in the air with a powered electricity, and I knew Diego was more than human.

"Are you a vampire?" The words spilled out of me.

If I'd asked that of anyone at the rave, they'd immediately say yes, but Diego considered me before answering.

"A demon is a demon no matter if they take blood or... something else."

My body started shaking. Breaths came in heaving swaths. My legs itched to move. Adrenaline dumped into my system making it hard to stay still, but I didn't have a doubt.

Diego was not human.

My bladder was ready to give out. My knees shook. The queasiness in my stomach churned, and my mouth started tasting acidic. I looked everywhere. Escape. Where was my car?

Diego's face went slack. The white sclera in his eyes turned black, and he swallowed.

"Don't run," he whispered.

I wanted nothing more than to hightail it out of here. Lilly had her own ride, and she was safe in the crowd. She didn't need me. Monsters lurked here.

No, Miles, I admonished myself. The little girl whose mother told her to run fast and far was now grown. I wouldn't die from blood loss, but I could still feel pain. I held firm and hid my quaking stomach. This could be my only chance to get the whereabouts of my mom.

"I'm your donor. I'll trade information—"

"What are you?" His face twisted in a snarl, the features morphing a little more angular. Claws, short and hooked, sprouted from his fingers, and he held his hands up to show me. "I don't have this reaction to just anyone."

I gritted my teeth. Did he try to compel me? Little prick. His I'm-so-innocent act pissed me off. How many victims succumbed to his pleasant demeanor and those innocent eyes? This was a true monster. "I could ask you the same thing."

"No." Diego leaned against the limo door and pointed in the opposite direction. "This is as far as you come. You're not getting your hands on him."

"What?" The adrenaline made me shake. Now I was angry. "You think I'm the danger?"

"Who sent you?" Diego's innocent mask faded into anger. "No," he chuffed. "I know who sent you. Tell that lying snake of a bitch that she's never going to get her hands on him. Not while I'm protecting him."

He obviously had me confused with someone else, but my fear turned to resentment. Attending this party for nothing wasn't an option. How much longer could my mom last? I'd been searching years for her. "I came here to trade for information."

"I'll pay you to leave." He snarled. "Name your price."

How did this turn into me being the monster? A bout of rage about toppled me over. I was not a flake. I was not a bloodsucker. I would do the job. Plus, Diego was the type of person—demon—I was looking for. "How about you answer some questions, then I'll go."

"One question. Then leave." Diego threw a clawed finger toward the crowd of people.

The window of the limo cracked part way, and a deep, slow, musky voice resonated power with a single word, "Diego."

The demon snapped his attention to the slit in the window. "I'm sorry, sir. We'll leave."

"No. Let Miss..." The voice floated into the air, and the man behind it waited for my name.

"Evans," Diego answered. "Miles Evans."

"Miles..." the voice said. My name over his tongue sounded erotic, enticing. "Come in if you like, but don't waste my aide's time. Diego is very busy."

The window went back up leaving me and this guy's aide staring at each other.

Diego cursed.

"It wasn't you this appointment was with?" I clenched my fists. Slow understanding dawned on me. Diego was here to bring me to this guy.

Oh, so careful with his words. Of course, Diego wouldn't hurt me. This was why demons were infuriating. Diego couldn't even be straight with me about who would imbibe my blood for information.

I needed to tread carefully. Vampire etiquette bore no resemblance to human conventions. Vampires were calculating. Patient. Economic at times. Easy to offend, and very deadly. Bottom line, even though I desperately wanted to know, there was no way I was going to ask who was in the limo. That would be offensive because it would be expected of me to know. Especially if he were an old vampire. And, no, it didn't make sense for a society that wanted to play itself on the down-low.

I was not keen on going inside, but a refusal might get my throat cut, which would be fine. I'd live. Or... come back alive at least. They might decide to scatter me into pieces. Not a boundary of my screwed-up "superpower" I wanted to test. Bleeding to death was fine. Piecing myself together... that was more undead territory.

Diego scowled at me then lifted two fingers and waved them in the universal code for "I'm watching you."

I huffed and stepped back.

Lord help me. When Diego opened the door, anger was the source of my strength as I climbed into the limo.

CHAPTER 2

THE INSIDE OF THE white stretched BMW was nothing like a typical party car for graduation. The usual long bench seat stretched down the long side and curved around the end. The opposite side sprouted a cubby-hole minibar, a screen, and a table. USB ports hid behind the plush white seats. Cords connected a laptop to the wall. The interior looked more like an underground office than a place to kick back while riding to the airport.

"Thank you for joining me, Ms. Evans." His voice vibrated inside me. Any college girl would bask in the rich, intoxicating vibe.

I gritted my teeth and focused on the man at the end of the limo. "A pleasure being here."

Skin, a pale sheen found only on walls and real vampires, contrasted with inky-black hair falling in a skillful artlessness long enough to blend into his black suit. A blood-red tie splashed the only color against the matching black shirt. High cheekbones, a straight nose, and thin lips could place him in almost any ethnicity. His red-gold eyes looked through me in a timeless stare.

What stopped my beating heart was the expression on his face. Overwhelming sadness. Lost hope. A warrior knowing he fought a meaningless war. One whose anger had bled out long ago leaving an empty shell of a man. The desolation he carried was palpable. Yet his voice remained immune to the silent, accepting misery within his eyes.

Those red-gold eyes watched in patient melancholy as I adjusted into the seat. He reminded me of a young corporate accountant, one that had seen enough soul-sucking depravity yet retained enough humanity to feel the wrongness of it all. Trapped, unable to extricate himself due to the contract he'd signed with the wrong corporation.

The door slammed, and I jumped at the force of movement. I jerked back keeping my eyes on the predator in the car. He might seem sad, but that didn't mean he didn't have to eat.

In my position, it was much better to show patience and say nothing than put my foot in my mouth. I waited him out in silence. Vampires liked to boast about themselves. All I had to do was give him time. Two minutes passed, and I neither moved nor looked away. Easy breaths measured my heart rate, but my mind raced.

I'd been catfished. Diego made our appointment for this man. Not himself. Now that I was in the car, I felt like a fool. They could drive away, and I'd be at their mercy. Never let it be said that human desperation couldn't surmount difficult choices. My mother was out there, being tortured by these monsters and if I wanted to get her out, I had to calm down, breathe, and trade for information.

I had to be careful. If they found out what I was, what I could do, then I could very well become a prisoner once again.

The man—vampire—lifted his hands and covered his mouth. "What can I do for you, Ms. Evans?"

The bottom of my stomach dropped, but it was now or never. "I don't believe we've been formally introduced."

If a real vampire was going to feed on me and leave me for dead, I wanted a name.

My question gave him pause, and his eyes shone in interest.

Perfect. The old ones were the worst to offend. They expected to be known, and I'd insulted him by not hearing about the great such and such.

Playing the waiting game wreaked havoc on my bladder. I blinked, and he was suddenly a foot closer, facing me with an arm slung over the back of the stretched seat.

Frayed nerves pumped even more adrenaline into my blood stream, and I inwardly cursed at my rising libido.

He tickled the ends of my fuchsia scarf and said, "My name is Warren Coroner."

Oh great, I'm totally dead. "Nice to meet you, Mr. Coroner."

My sincerity would have been convincing had my voice not cracked.

His eyes studied me until he filtered everything he could from my reaction. In a slow, exaggerated cadence, Warren asked, "Why are you here, Ms. Evans?"

"In-information." I fumbled with the knot in my scarf.

Warren's eyes fixated on my clumsy fingers until I removed the accessory and exposed my abused throat. I knew what he saw. A neck under siege of human bite marks with a colorful bloom of abuse. The night before, I'd let a newbie wannabe vampire gnaw on my neck for rent money. Because I'm not a masochist, I didn't enjoy it. But an orphan's gotta live so...

His nose flared, and his throat bobbed. Twin flames burned in his eyes making him look more alive... and angry.

"I'll trade," I continued, with a stuttering voice. "I need to find someone."

"Get out," Warren said.

"What?"

"Get out!"

"But I—"

"Diego!" he growled.

"No! Wait!" I lurched forward and grabbed hold of the lapels of his suit, our faces inches apart.

Warren narrowed his eyes, burrowing his glowing glare into me, and said, "Do you want to die?"

I had to be careful. If I asked for my mom directly, he probably wouldn't know who she was at all. I'd ask for the last person I'd seen her with before my escape. "Eli Florentine. Tell me where he is."

"Diego!" Warren yelled.

I'd grown up too fast. A normal child had innocence. Not me. It was as if I were born knowing more about vampire nature from instinct. Diego sent me in here to die. That much I knew, but Warren's reaction was curious.

"He's not coming," I said. "Diego is the one that set this meeting up."

"What?" He drew back, as if I were the danger, but I held on to his jacket and didn't let go. My head bumped the top of the soft limo ceiling, and the strain of holding on to him tore at the scabs along my arms from last night's feeding. I found myself sitting on top of him at the back of the limo.

Warren closed his eyes and whispered, "I don't want this."

Well, buddy, I sure as hell don't want to be here either. I drew another breath and turned my head to the side, revealing the unblemished part of my neck. "I'm trading information for blood."

Pale eyelids snapped open. Calculating, he examined me. "You are a beautiful woman, Ms. Evans," he ground out. "But you need to get off me, right now."

No way. Not without something for my time. "Tell me where Eli Florentine is, and I'll go."

His nose crinkled in distaste, baring his pointed canines at me.

Careful. Your vampire is showing.

In a flash, his sneer dropped into a blank expression. Eyes fixed on my neck, canine teeth elongated, holding me in place, Warren stared.

That look was never a good sign. I had seconds before the vampire would strike. I staved down the panic to reach for the laser pointer. It had saved me before, and it was all I had not to reach for it, but I had no time. One moment I was holding on to the suit of Warren Coroner, the next I was surrounded by black smoke.

The man had vaporized. I fell into the seat he'd been in and turned around. A dark cloud billowing like a cumulus in slow motion gathered in the limo. Smoke bloomed into multiple undulating cauliflower heads.

Holy crap! Warren was obviously a very old, very strong being. He could strike from anywhere. Terror held me immobile.

A wide black snout with jagged canines poked through the cloud. It was as if dark clouds were the body of the beast and the only things solid were his nose, mouth, and teeth.

"Tell me where Eli Florentine is!"

The lion muzzle rushed forward, and the dark, heavy mist followed.

Pain bloomed over my throat. His bite excruciating. I tried to push it away, but my hands only scattered smoke. Move, Miles!

I pushed myself to the car door. The thing latched onto my neck swallowed pints of my life away. My mind whirled. My heart pumped faster, compensating for the thinning blood pressure. Chest pain ripped out my strength. Heart attack. I would die. Death was never pleasant. I advise against it.

The human body holds about a gallon of blood. But this demon sucked faster than anything I'd known. The black tunnel of unconsciousness narrowed my vision. Even as the demon drained me and I was falling under the spell of shock, a soothing calm spread through my veins. My fingers reached for the laser pointer in my jeans pocket.

My consciousness was fading, but I took hold of the pen and pulled it free.

A shining red light flashed, and then the world went black.

Chapter 3

THE USUAL HAZE of waking up after death didn't plague me. I lay flat on my back.

Warmth settled over my skin. A breeze skimmed over my face. I didn't want to open my eyes. Maybe I was really and truly dead.

A soft, melodious voice said, "Miles..."

Noooo... this is the best sleep I've gotten since... ever. I palmed soft grass and doggedly ignored the call of my name.

"Miles, I know you're conscious."

Birds called in the distance. I turned on my side and scrunched myself into a ball. This was so nice. Why wake up?

"Chamomile!"

I gasped and sat up to find a kindly old man kneeling over me. His hands clasped together as if in prayer. His gentle smile enhanced his trim gray beard, making me feel at ease. The man's short white hair styled in a windblown coif, happy, crystal blue eyes, and a broad nose screamed priest.

"I know you like to be called Miles." He flashed a sympathetic smile. "We were eager to speak with you."

I'd shuddered whenever people called me Chamomile, but off his lips it felt natural.

"Okay." Dubious of his intent, I looked at him. "You know that name how?"

The man spread his arms wide. "Be not afraid, Chamomile Makayla Evans Eirian."

He knew my name. My full real name. Where was I? What had I been doing before this?

"How do you know my name?"

Behind him in the distance, fog settled revealing an expanse of green grass and trees. We were in a clearing with gnarled oaks standing guard in a circle around us. It was rather uncanny how symmetrical they were in size and spacing.

"Where are we?" I twisted around. Among the circle of sentries, I saw a face hidden within the branches. I couldn't tell if it was a man or woman.

Mister Priest before me remained kneeling as if he could be in that position all day.

"Welcome to the Brightwood Estate," he said.

Huh? "So, how far is it from my car?"

The man laughed. "Quite a ways, my dear. May I call you 'Miles'?'" He paused and returned his gentle smile.

I narrowed my eyes. Who was this guy? "So, you know my name. What's yours?"

"I have many names." His voice trailed like that of an old sage getting ready to tell a story. "But you can call me Michael."

"Great. Michael. Why am I here? Who's this 'we' that wanted to talk to me?"

He patted his chest. "We are both here."

Okay, so he meant the royal we. This guy was a little out there. I'd met a few like him. They looked normal enough but when you started talking to them, that's when the strange came out. Considering I didn't know where I was and wanted to get out of here, I'd play nice.

Michael stood up, and his long white robe swayed as his arm swept over in a gesture to a curved stone bench that had not been there a moment ago. "Come. Sit."

I got up and followed him to the half-circle seat. It felt like concrete on my ass. When I first woke up, I had my reservations as to whether this was a dream or not. The verdict was still out.

Michael stared at the ground as if lost in thought, giving me a chance to sincerely see him. His worry lines were faint, but the rest of his face gave a youthful appearance. He reminded me of some movie monk with his off-white linen robe and windswept hair. His kindness shone through his eyes. Even with his bizarre behavior, something about this man made me at ease.

Michael snapped out of his reverie and said, "I see my... Warren has taken to you."

"You mean the straight outta Compton Balrog?"

His trim eyebrows rose. "That's a new one. I've never heard him called that before."

"How about fog monster? Or stone-cold killer, because if I'm not mistaken, I'm dead right now."

"I see you don't think very highly of him." Michael's eyebrows pinched together. "I suppose he didn't make a very good first impression."

Was that shame in his eyes? "What's it to you?"

"He's important to us."

Did I insult Warren to his family? "Is there a reason he needed to make a good first impression on me?"

Michael faced me. Within his eyes was... something. Something beyond Michael. Something within him. An other type of something.

"Perhaps you can love him someday."

"Love him? You mean Warren? How? What for?"

Worry features on the priest's face seemed foreign, as if he never worried much about anything.

"Are you religious, Miles?"

Whoa. Conversation whiplash. "I haven't actually thought about it."

"You know there are vampires. Why not believe in God?"

That question made me angry. "Why should I?"

"Have you read any of the scriptures?" Michael challenged.

"Oh, I get it. You're my subconscious, and you're here to mentally prepare me for heaven. I'm really dead, aren't I? I'm not coming back." This was it. I'd found the limit to my immortality.

Michael laughed. "You're a curious one, Miles."

"Kettle calling the pot black," I murmured.

"You're not dead." Michael's eyes twinkled in merriment. "I was asking because it's what I always ask."

It was hard to keep being the snarky tough girl with Michael's loving gaze and fatherly warmth. A part of me wanted to bury my face in his robes and cry out my frustrations. I had this sense he would understand.

"Come, child." Michael pulled me into his embrace. "Be not distraught. All is well."

Had anyone held me with such kindness?

Never.

Before I knew it, hot wetness streamed down my face. Tears of relief whisked my torment away. Everything was going to be fine.

We sat there for who knows how long. It could have taken ten years for me to stop crying. Time seemed endless, irrelevant, or nonexistent.

"Miles?" Michael took my shoulders and gently pushed me back.

I swiped at my tears. "Yeah?"

"Take a look, listen, and know." Michael pointed down.

I expected to see dirt or clouds or something other than an overhead view of Warren Coroner hovering over a linen sheet. Diego was opposite of him, and I could hear their conversation.

"Don't torture yourself like this," Diego said. "It was a mistake."

"Why, Diego?" Warren bowed his head over a figure wrapped in a beige sheet. "I don't understand you sometimes."

Diego struggled with words, and he reached out to touch Warren, but his hand hovered as if thinking better than touching him. "I'm sorry. It's... you starve yourself for what?"

"I want to protect them, not..." Warren buried his face in the crook of his arm.

Michael laid a hand on my shoulder. "Warren is troubled over you, child."

"He should be. He ate me."

"Are you sure that's what he wanted to do?"

I tsked. "Isn't that what all vampires want to do?"

Michael didn't so much as frown as let his smile fade. "Perhaps you could try to get to know the inheritor better."

As sexy and tempting as Warren was, I was going to have to disappoint the priest. "Perhaps another hug might help me think about it."

The priest laughed and grabbed hold of me again. I didn't want to leave this warmth and watched from the comfort of his arms.

Warren set a hand on the sheet, and I noticed details like shadows on the linen in the form of a body.

"I don't know what came over me," Warren whispered. "I haven't ever felt such burning need before."

"She was different." Diego set light fingers on Warren's hand. "I knew I shouldn't have let her in the car."

Warren gently squeezed Diego's hand. "Leave me be."

"I'll be quiet, but I'm not leaving you alone." Diego pulled back and sat in the first-row pew of what looked like a small town church.

Warren tucked the sheet under the body's arm and slid his long, thin fingers over the body's palm.

I could feel the sensation of my own hand being held.

"I'm sorry," he whispered so low I wasn't sure anyone else could hear him. "It's no consolation, but I have no other words."

"Miles…" Michael embraced me a little tighter. "You have to go back now."

"Don't wanna." I grabbed tighter onto Michael's robes.

He laughed and hugged me closer. "Remember this moment, Chamomile. Remember this feeling and know that even the inheritor needs this."

"Who?"

He gave me another of his smiles, and I could feel the light shining from him.

"Wait!" I grabbed for Michael, but it was as if my arms were smoke. They passed right through him.

"You are not alone, Miles. Can you remember that?"

"Can't I stay here a bit longer?" Waking up after being drained was always hell.

Michael smiled, gentle. "He would like to see you with his own eyes."

"Is he Warren?"

Another broad smile and laugh. Then Michael opened his mouth impossibly wide, and sitting at the back of his throat was a pair of iridescent eyes. They were beautiful and terrifying but radiated love. I was blasted with a sense of calm even as I sank into an abyss of nothing. The weight of an ocean pulled me into darkness, yet I didn't fear it. Wrapped in a warm cocoon, I went back to sleep.

CHAPTER 4

I HATED WHEN I woke up dead.

This time, it was nothing like my dream. Consciousness swam to the surface hauling me from drunken blood loss. My arms and legs weighed as much as steel pipes and didn't budge when I tried to move. Opening my eyes meant getting the weight of a rhino off my lids. The only thing working was my voice. Barely.

A soft and low moan vibrated my teeth. I could feel my lips quiver, but forming words was a challenge.

Small, consistent breaths helped oxygenate life in my veins. I was awake, which meant I'd recovered from blood loss. How long I'd been out would be determined by how many of Lilly's texts I'd missed.

Scratchy fabric resisted the efforts of my wiggling finger. The air felt stale. The clothes I wore were not my own, but I didn't smell the telltale chemicals of a morgue, yet it was silent as death.

No matter how many times, I'll never get used to waking up on a cold metal table and startled morticians. A note in my purse labeled "In case of my death" left specific instructions to not embalm, cremate, or perform an autopsy on me. I was to be laid out and left alone. Preferably in the shade. Unfortunately, no one ever wanted to lay a dead body under a tree. Go figure.

It was cases like this that made me paranoid. I did not want scars or to find out what happened when I woke up with embalming fluid. Since it was my blood that resurrected me, cremation would certainly kill me.

Times like these also made me wonder if Jesus were like me. Coming back after a three-day dirt nap was a point in my corner for yes. Though I supposed the theory of vampire applied too, but I was not a vampire. I was something else.

Strength seeped into my bones, and my senses became more aware. I opened my eyes to—beige.

Linen covered my body. Best case scenario, someone thought I was cold—all the way up to my ears. More likely, they thought I was dead. Either way, I was taking off the itchy covering.

I rose, pawing the sheet off my face. A crucifix stared back at me. Thank goodness, I was in an open air on a slab. It felt like marble.

The chapel-like setting was small. Humble. Personable. As if I'd woken in a mini church. A stained glass window, the size of a medieval castle tower, cast soft lighting onto the cross. The size could have been affected by my angle and the spinning in my head.

Three rows of pews centered the room. Diego sat in the front with his head bowed, eyes closed, and hands clasped together in silent prayer.

I didn't want to disturb him. If I were super quiet, I could sneak past him and be off as if this whole affair was over. As if I hadn't been eaten by a Balrog from Lord of the Rings.

Slowly, I swung my legs down and laid the sheet aside.

That's when I noticed a tug on my other hand. I looked and saw the shocked red-gold eyes and gaping mouth of the very monster of ash and fire that had eaten me.

Warren Coroner stared at me, and he was holding my right hand with both of his own. His grip was light and tender. In his eyes, I saw shame, regret, and concern. We watched each other, me in abject horror, him in this shocked hope.

The dimness of the limo had done him no justice. If he weren't a bloodsucker, he'd have been a girl's wet dream. Strong jaw, aquiline nose, severe cheekbones, flawless skin wrapped in the sophistication of royalty.

He looked dumbfounded. Ha! I, Miles Evans, could make a big, strong demon of the echelon confounded.

The linen at my side dropped to the floor with a noisy whoosh.

Diego raised his head, and his blank stare met my gaze.

He blinked. Then again, blinked.

Uh-oh. His face resembled the scared disbelief of a mortician I'd freaked out. Before I could reach out and tell him not to... Diego screamed.

At the top of his lungs and with the enthusiasm of a twelve-year-old girl, he yelled like a thriller victim. His wild, high-pitched screams echoed in the mini church. Diego thrashed backward into the second and third row of pews like I was one of the four horsemen of the apocalypse.

Disbelief rooted my butt to the table. Here was the guy—a demon—who worked for the sexiest and most vicious beast I'd ever seen, and he was frantic because I'd woken up? Granted he thought I was dead, but still, he worked for a force of darkness and evil. Shouldn't he be used to strange things like this?

"What is your problem?" I pulled my hand free of Warren and set both on my hips.

"Warren!" Diego's voice cracked at the last syllable splitting his screaming to a high-pitched wail. "What is she?"

"Hold on..." My hands rose in supplication. "Hold on..."

Diego cried out louder.

I jumped off the stone slab and searched for my shoes. No such consideration of footwear was left for me, but at least I had on a clean T-shirt and cloth pants. Dang. Where was my phone?

The flutter of wings, a shift in the air, and master and servant jumped together to the back of the pews. Diego was in front, his stance that of a protector, acting like I'd attack his charge. Behind him stood the tallest, sexiest man that had been holding my hand just a moment ago. Warren had to reach seven feet. Me being five foot nine meant I saw eye to eye with most guys, but he made me feel petite even from fifteen feet away.

Diego swallowed, holding a sword in one shaking hand, a gun in the other. Where the heck did he get those? I couldn't blame the kid. He thought I was a walking corpse. I thought I'd better say something, before I got shot.

"I can explain." My hands rose in defense.

Diego firmed his stance, choosing the gun and sheathing the sword. "What do I do, boss?"

Warren snarled and pushed Diego behind him. "Stay back, Diego. She's dangerous."

"You." I pointed at Warren. He looked—different. Kept. Not so sad and homeless. "You ate me!" Not that it wasn't the deal I was trying to make, but he hadn't given me the information I wanted. "Pay up."

That last part sounded better in my head. I guess a corpse rising and saying, "You owe me" might be taken as threatening.

"You were dead." Diego peeked out from behind his monster-shield, still pointing the gun at me, and adjusted his glasses. "He killed you."

"Not very well," Warren said, eyeing me, and pushing Diego back. His red-gold eyes tracking my every movement. "Perhaps I should try again."

"Whoa! Whoa! Whoa! Don't get greedy." I knew better than to run or make fast movements. This wasn't the only time I'd freaked someone out because of a DOA situation, but trying to keep me dead was a first.

"How is she standing here like flies hadn't been buzzing around her for three days?" Diego asked from behind his guard.

Eww. A long recovery meant more blood taken. No wonder I was still tired. I was also starving. "You took every last drop, didn't you?"

Diego looked up to Warren. "Right? You killed her? You didn't make her some golem?"

Warren side-eyed his assistant. "You know that's not something I do."

"I knew it!" Diego sneered at me. "Nothing but a demon could bring her back."

"Or a miracle," Warren countered.

They both stared at me, and I let them process. The silence grew. Even with my laser pointer, I wouldn't be able to cut the tension between us.

Warren, the thing masquerading as human, sniffed the air. "How are you alive?"

"Ummm... luck?" I gave a half-hearted smile.

The large demon leveled his gaze at me. "A second recovery for you would be doubtful."

I may be special with a capital "S" but not so much I could live through a beheading, cremation, or impaling my heart.

Warren had speed. If he went for me again, I wouldn't be able to stop him. I didn't feel like I had a choice. My secret was also my freedom. Death wasn't the liberation I was looking for right now. My chances were better being caged and used for what I'd been bred to be—a blood doll. Maybe. That meant I would have to reveal my secret.

Warren shifted his weight. Not a lot, but enough to know that his patience waned.

"I... I have an artifact!" I searched with my hands over my body, but all I had on was an off-white gown. "It gives me another life." Like a video game talisman.

"Oh..." Diego relaxed. "That makes sense."

Warren pressed a palm to his chest as if a blow had struck his heart. His eyes flicked to me and growled, "Don't lie."

Before I knew what happened, Warren came face-to-face with me. He was close enough for me to lick his nose.

"What are you?" He narrowed his eyes. "Tell me true or die. Permanently."

If I were dead, then my mom had no hope. "I'm a blood doll."

My blurted confession didn't have the effect I wanted, which was him stepping away from me. Instead, recognition glittered in Warren's eyes.

"Blood doll," Diego huffed. "That's a new term for a donor."

"Blood dolls don't exist," Warren hissed.

"Do blood slaves come back from being completely drained?" I asked.

Warren narrowed his eyes in an intense focused glower. "We don't have blood slaves."

I laughed. Truly, genuinely laughed. Vampires always had blood slaves. They subsisted on them. Every enclave had blood slaves, or blood escorts or whatever they called them now. The poor souls that were kept alive until a vampire fed from them. "Sure, you don't."

"He doesn't have blood slaves," Diego grumbled, examining his shoes. "It's the reason..."

"Sanderson," Warren hissed, turning his gaze away from me.

Diego squared his shoulders back in challenge. "You know something. Tell me."

Neither Warren nor I spoke. We clashed in a contest of will. The first that talked lost. Information was a commodity more precious than money. Time wasn't a factor for demons. They were indestructible. Forever. Many held grudges for centuries. Power and information were timeless currencies demons never abandoned.

"Hello?" Diego waved his hands. "Anyone care to explain what the difference between a blood doll and a blood slave is?"

Warren spoke, slowly albeit, but still first to break the silence. "A blood doll is a creature so rare that blood users stopped talking about them an era ago."

Ha! I won the silence contest.

The tension in the air lifted and was replaced by a different type of intensity. I was a blood doll. Warren was a blood drinker. I was as rare as finding the heart of a star in a pile of rubble. If he wanted, he could cage me and drain me over and over until the end of time, or the end of my life, whichever came first. I'd be trapped and unable to find my mother. She'd fought so hard to get me away from one hell that I wouldn't let her sacrifice go to waste.

Diego looked at me, looked at Warren, adjusted his glasses then said in an overly sweet tone, "Oh, yeah, sure. That clears everything up. Let me get the tea and cookies, and we can all have a chat about..." He raised his voice. "What the hell is a blood doll!"

The right corner of Warren's right eye flinched, but a slight curve thinned his lips.

I was both amused and frustrated by Diego's antics. "I can recover to full function after being"—I put emphasis on the last word—"drained."

We waited for Diego to get it. Any moment, the wheels of his brain would turn, and then I'd get an offer I couldn't refuse. That's how it worked with these types. They never thought about my freedom. They started with "You need protection. Dangerous monsters roam out there."

Never did any of them think that maybe I didn't want them to use my neck as a pincushion. Selling my blood was one thing. Being forced to donate for "my own good" was another.

"Wait, wait, wait." Diego did an equivalent to jazz hands only trying to wave off his confusion. "You can lose all the blood in your body and then recover?"

"My heart remakes it. I don't understand the science behind it. It just works. No matter how many times all the blood in my body is drained, my body replenishes it."

Dang it. Why was I running my mouth... Oh, the little bastard was good. I glared at Diego and his suggestibility power.

"Like a refillable pez dispenser?" Diego cocked his head.

Warren snarled at Diego. "Respect, please."

"Sorry." Diego came forward.

Warren pointed at Diego. "Don't—"

"Don't what?" The smaller man adjusted his glasses. "Oh!" Diego looked at me and understanding spread over his smiling face. Sharks were more inviting than Mr. Innocent right now. His eyes gleamed in greedy acknowledgment like a banker selling junk bonds.

"Miles." His voice dripped with sweetness so thick it would give me diabetes listening to him.

"No," Warren said. "Take her back to wherever she wants."

My gasp of air went unnoticed. Go? I could go? No, this was a trick. I wanted so badly to ask where I could find Eli Florentine. First rule of negotiations, come from a place of power. This was not where I was strongest. If I pushed, how good would the knowledge be if I were enslaved?

"Let's think about this." Diego raised his palms.

"My answer is no." Warren walked to the base of stairs beyond the pews.

"But... she'll never die. You could be... normal. You'd never starve."

"I will not be responsible for her." Warren gave his assistant a glare so terrifying it was sexy. Only because he was letting me go though. Was I free? There was a catch. There was always a catch.

"You already are responsible for her!" Diego thrust his hands wildly at me.

Warren snarled, "Blood dolls are everything wrong in the world. They cause wars. They have no mercy. Their hunger for power is greater than even a demon's hunger for blood."

What. The. Ever. Loving. Heck. Everything wrong in the world? Sure I was a rare commodity, but I was used, caged and drained. Over and over. I was the victim. It hurt my heart to think someone, even a merciless demon, might think I could seek power. I just wanted my mother back.

Warren gripped the railing and took a long, suffering sigh. "She wants to leave. Let her go."

"But out there... she's not safe." Diego started whining like a kid that wasn't allowed a new toy. "She should stay."

Of course. There it was. I was a pretty little butterfly that couldn't defend herself.

"I'm not safe anywhere," I chimed in. "Hasn't stopped me yet."

Warren nodded and slowly ascended the stairs.

"Seriously, she could... attract others."

By others, Diego meant other demons. I could be used as demon bait. Once it was known a blood doll was out there, monsters would start crawling out of hell to get to me. No thank you to that whole nerve-wracking scenario.

Diego looked at me, cringed, and mouthed, sorry as though he'd thought about what he'd said after the fact.

Too tired to care I shrugged and sighed. It was true. Hating someone for speaking the truth was like admonishing a person for being brave.

"This would make our job easier," Diego called after him.

His words didn't deter Warren. The seven-foot demon kept climbing the stairs.

Diego turned to me, masking his inner evil accountant with innocence. "Name your price."

I scoffed. "I'll take freedom every day."

"He needs someone like you." Diego threw his hands at the ascending demon. "These past few days he's been focused. Powerful. No one is his match when he's like this."

Warren's snarl echoed off the stairway hall. Typical, but that was a demon. Calling any of them weak was cause for proving themselves otherwise. Fastest way to get into a brawl? Tell a vampire they were powerless.

The remarkable part was, Diego still had his heart in his own chest after his accusation. Warren had a lot of restraint, or Diego could hold his own. The jury was still out.

"Diego," Warren's scary-sexy voice filtered down from the hallway. "Take her to where she wants to go. Then we will talk about your subterfuge."

Diego gulped. Verdict settled. Warren had restraint.

I heard Warren stomping up the stairs. He didn't come back down. I'd been left alone with his underling. As I recalled, Diego wasn't a bloodsucker, but he wasn't human either. I palmed my trusty laser pointer. It worked on humans and demons alike.

I jumped down from the altar and started looking for an exit. All I saw were the stairs.

Diego took off his glasses, rubbed his eyes, and returned his frames to his face. "I'm sorry," he sighed. "You must hate me."

"Oh no, not really." My words were entirely sarcastic. "You lured me away from the crowd, kidnapped me, stuffed me in your car, then fed me to your master. I don't hate you."

My body stiffened. I'd have to fight with my fists and my feet to get out of here because now that Diego knew what I was, he'd never let me go.

Diego slumped forward looking dejected.

Nope. I am never falling for that act again.

"You're right," he said. "I was desperate. I knew he was falling apart. I should've done something sooner."

I said nothing and crept toward the stairs while facing him but angling myself so I could turn and run.

"Miles, for what it's worth, I'm sorry." He looked up, pleading.

"Sorry doesn't cut it. You used up one of my lives."

He perked up at that. "Do you only have a certain number of times you can be drained?"

"I'm not playing tit for tat with you." But maybe I could get information out of him. Because if I wasn't trapped here, I wanted to find my mother.

Diego adjusted his glasses and shifted to face me. "Fine. I'll take you wherever you want to go."

"I'm not going anywhere with you."

He lifted his eyebrows then grimaced. "I deserve that, but there's one small problem."

"What?"

"You're on an island. Care to swim across the Pacific? Or do you know how to fly a Blackhawk?" He waved his hand. "Go ahead, I give you two minutes before one of the ferals chases you back behind the gates."

Where the hell was I? "Explain."

"You're on an island. For a mortal, the only way out is by air lift. Oh, and there are some freaky creatures roaming outside the gates, so getting to the lakeshore unescorted is fairly insane. In case you want to swim."

"No boat?"

"Yeah, no boat. We can't have any of the ferals boarding it and getting over to the mainland."

What the hell was a feral?

Diego was smiling to himself and shaking his head in remembrance. "That was a wild night."

I was almost to the stairs and ready to make a break for it. Screw this intimidation talk. I was getting out of here.

"Miles..." Power rippled through Diego's voice. "Please don't run."

A wave of reason and logic as to why I shouldn't turn tail and scramble out of here blasted my thoughts. I didn't know where I was. Diego might be telling the truth. I was on an island. Who knew what kind of house this was and where I would find an exit?

Logic hadn't stopped me before, but it'd given Diego enough time to step in front of me and block my path.

"Miles, I know I haven't given you any reason to trust me, but I didn't mean for any of this to happen. You were supposed to be a pint for a night and returned to your home." His eyes pleaded with me to believe him. "Please give me the chance to take you back. I'll take you anywhere you want."

"Anywhere?"

He nodded.

"Then take me to my mother, asshole."

Diego adjusted his glasses and said, "Okay, where is she?"

A decade's worth of frustration, desperation, and soul-crushing loss crumpled my face into a mask of unbidden tears. I palmed my eyes as I tried to force the waterworks back. Another mission of trying to find her gone wrong. The vampire rave was supposed to be my break. I was going to find someone who knew about my mother. I was supposed to find her.

"Oh God, Miles? I'll take you. I'll take you anywhere you want. Just tell me where. If she's in Istanbul, I'll get you there." Diego handed me a tissue. Where he got it from, I had no clue. When I looked into his dark eyes, I found compassion. Our hands touched, and his slim fingers were warm and comforting. My heart lifted a little. I didn't know if that was due to his nonhuman powers or if it was because it had been a long time since anyone cared enough to give me a Kleenex.

"You're such a simp." My voice quivered.

He smiled in gracious chagrin. "That's me. It's sort of a prerequisite for my kind."

Nope. Not going to ask what his kind was, more because he wanted me to ask.

Crying wasn't going to help me find my mother, though, and I had this opportunity to maybe find her. I took a deep breath and asked, "You'll take me anywhere?"

Diego picked up on the subtlety of my question and raised a dark eyebrow, making him look scrumptiously wicked. He wasn't my type, but he had some heavy mojo all the same.

"I can take you to coordinates, a zip code, cross streets, a place, but I can't take you to a place I don't know, or to a person I don't know."

"What about Eli Florentine?"

Diego shot me a teacher's glare. Everyone knows that look. Diego stared at me over his glasses as they perched low on his nose. "If I knew where Eli Florentine was, his soul would've been ripped from that body a while ago."

I let the breath I held go. Better luck next time. Story of my life. "Fine. I want to go home."

"Great." He smiled, but it was a politician's grin. It still would charm the pants off so many coeds I knew. "Where is home?"

"The Rusty Teapot."

"Okay." He nodded. "That I can do."

The Rusty Teapot was a diner below an apartment building. All the wannabe vamps worth their salt collected there. I'd scored one of the apartments above it knowing I might cross the path of someone who knew about real vampires.

"Follow me." Diego turned and made his way up the stairs.

Small paintings littered the hallway wall following the stairwell. Some pictures depicted scenes of war in orange and red hues. Others were the exact opposite with flower fields in bright blue, yellow, green, and pink. The texture grabbed my eye making me want to smell the flowers, but as I climbed, I came to one larger canvas framed by other smaller pictures in a cascade effect that showed an epic battle.

In the middle of the smaller paintings, an armor-clad angel floated above the ground, pointing his sword in challenge. Blond hair waved in the air as if a strong breeze pushed the angel's locks away from his face. His eyes, bright and determined, focused on a single point. In the background was a gruesome scene of dead demons littering the ground. All of them were slaughtered, except one.

The angel pointed his silver sword, eyes ablaze, judgement upon his face, wings extended in fierce challenge to the last remaining demon.

Kneeling before the angel, sword pointed to the ground, the hilt sliding out from the demon's loose grasp, and though the demon's face wasn't shown, his spirit conveyed elation, relief, uncertainty and awe worthy of the main subject floating in the air.

Mercy poured out to the subjugated demon, but the angel... I felt like I'd known him all my life. It was as though his sword pointed at me, and his eyes of judgement challenged me to be a better person.

"I think that's his best one." Diego stood five steps above watching me assess the painting.

I scanned the others telling a story of redemption. One depicted the demon standing in awe before the angel. Supplication. "Wait, who did these?"

Diego glanced at the one I was staring at. "Warren."

I waved at the collage of images. "He painted these?"

"He painted all of them." Diego waved his hand to the whole wall. Pictures of a man and woman that resembled Adam and Eve, impressionist battles, and lifelike portraits hung there in splendor. They were all beautiful. All deserving a place in a museum.

Talented demon.

Diego did an about face and continued up the stairs.

With a lingering look, I pulled away from the paintings and carried on upward.

The next floor was more ostentatious than the humble temple below.

Large windows, a loose curved staircase that split in opposite directions, and marble floors screamed foyer fit for a prince. It was clean but cold. Very elitist. A home worthy of intimidation and a show of power. Much like any vampire would want.

My bare feet hit the cool marble floor, and a chill shuddered down my spine. "Is this the second story?" I couldn't get my bearings. Was the chapel in a basement?

"Stay close." Diego walked, and I followed.

He stopped abruptly and swung his arm out to keep me from going forward. Diego tilted his head like a dog listening to some humanly incomprehensible sound. He turned at a ninety-degree angle and walked. "This way."

"What the heck?" I murmured.

"Sorry, my dear. The house is a bit Escher."

Whatever. I followed him to the opulent marble stairs.

"All right, Miles. Take a step, just one step and face me." He stretched his arm out with the flair of a Latin lover and hung his hand in the air, waiting for me to take it.

He looked... different. It was still Diego, but he didn't look like a kid anymore. The attention-sucking black eyes were the same soft wells of inky sincerity, but his cheekbones were higher, his mouth adorned a sinful smile promising mischief, and his looks were now the type of person I might date—if I had a real life. I took his hand because who wouldn't want to touch a stallion like him.

Then I mentally shook myself and gave him a pointed glare. "Stop it."

He feigned innocence. "Stop what?"

"That whole thing you do." I gestured a hand to him.

"Why wave at my face? Don't you like it?" His megawatt smile lit up the room.

"Who are you?" I removed my hand.

"I'm Diego. Diego Sanderson." As if he were a double-o spy.

"Oh, my stars." The sexiness also dripped with cheese.

He took both my hands in his and brought my knuckles to his heart. "Stay here, darling. Promise?"

"Wait, where are you going?" Anxiety vibrated through me thinking he was going to leave me here in this huge house. A house that reminded me too much of my early life with vampires.

He leaned closer to me. "I'll be right back. Just going down the hall for a bit. It's safer if you stay here."

I glanced at our entwined hands. "Diego, you're freaking me out."

"Sorry." He let go of my hands and backed away. "You're nervous. It's instinct for me to comfort you."

So he can eat me. "Uh-huh."

Where was that hospitality in the chapel?

"Stay here, no matter what you see, all right?" His big soft eyes pleaded.

"Fine."

"Great!" He zoomed off down the hall, side-stepping whole areas. I couldn't see what he was avoiding. For all I knew, there were traps on the floor.

He vanished down a hall, and my stomach plummeted as a shadow fell behind me in the empty foyer. I turned around to see a huge cathedral-shaped window. A picturesque skyscape of clouds floating in the blue sky soared toward the sun. It was gorgeous. If this was what Warren saw every day, no wonder he wanted to capture it on canvas. This was a muse-inspiring nature scene. Nebulous, puffy white clouds crept across the sky, in front of the sun, blocking its rays.

The hair along my neck lifted, and I got the sense someone was watching me. I could see the entire foyer, but little scuffles and whispers echoed off the marble beyond sight. My body vibrated, like I should run, and my hands trembled. The whispers got louder.

"Hello?" I called out.

No answer. But the whispers continued.

Crap. I started biting my nails, doing anything to release the building anxiety of waiting. Diego said I would be safe, but how much could I trust someone that led me to be a snack for his boss. I was such a fool.

The murmurs became words, or rather a name. My name. A female staccato called out to me in a faint wheeze. Miles... Miles... I'm here, Miles...

I caught my breath. "Mom?"

As the cloud cover blotted the sun and the foyer got a lot darker, I listened for an answer.

Miles... Miles, come here, my Miles...

"Mom?" I leaned forward to step off the stairs and rush to her side when a foot slammed down on tile.

I jumped, causing me to lose my balance. I was going to bust my butt on these stairs, and I could do nothing about it.

A streak flashed, and Warren was behind me, preventing my fall. "Easy." Warren held my wrists, keeping me upright. "Keep your feet on this step."

"Ack!" I felt a little embarrassed. Damsel in distress.

Warren raised his head and stared out into the foyer and growled deep and low. It sent a chill down my spine.

Something skittered across the floor, and a chittering laugh echoed off the tile. Tiny clicking, like metal tapping on marble, scuttled out of the room taking the darkness with it.

"Are you lost?" Warren let my wrists go. "Where is Diego?"

Frightened, embarrassed, and tired, all I had to go on was anger. "What the heck was that?"

Red-gold eyes shone with intensity. "What did you hear?"

Tread lightly, Miles. This being was part of the echelon. The elite. A monster on top of the food chain. A being that could transform into smoke and strike out was best treading around carefully.

Warren backed away, taking one step down, and my forehead almost reached up to his shoulders. It gave me a good chance to look at his handsome features up close. The brightness in his eyes dulled. The sorrow I'd seen when we first met returned.

"It's fine if you don't want to say." Warren turned away. "I'd rather you not think of ways to lie to me."

"My mother," I blurted out. "I heard my mother."

He turned back to me, and we stood in silence. He searched my face as if looking for something. I wasn't sure if he found it, but I'd answered him truthfully.

"I guarantee you it was not her." His lips thinned.

Figures. Whatever badie mimicked my mother laughed at me on its way out.

"I came to apologize," he said. "I realized I did not give you proper reparation."

Oh. It was the first time a blood drinker said I'm sorry to me. It took me aback. How much damage did his pride take apologizing to me, a human? Rejecting his apology or making light of it was another faux pas most humans didn't understand about vampire culture.

"Words are a novelty, but I expect to be paid." I'd been drained of all my blood before, but it didn't mean I was used to the pain of dying and the recovery after. I swallowed my trauma and tried for businesslike. "Next time I need notice and a time when I can take a few days to recover."

Warren blinked and stared at me like he didn't know what to do with me. Did I get it wrong? Should I have said apology accepted?

Rushing footsteps came down the hall, and Diego emerged with a coat and shoes. "Took me a minute to find your size... oh! Sir, I will take her now."

"Sanderson." Warren cast a stern eye to his assistant.

Diego's Adam's apple bobbed. "Uh, yes, sir?"

"You left her unattended inside of Brightwood."

"She has no shoes, and she should have a coat where she's going." Diego held up the items in his arms.

"You left a human alone in Brightwood," Warren explained like he was talking to a child that should know better.

Diego's eyebrows lifted from behind his thick-framed glasses. "You wanted me to bring a human further into Brightwood?"

"I suppose not." Warren sighed.

For me, this was an interesting exchange. I was so used to vampires using violence to get the message across, but Diego didn't seem fearful toward Warren, more like he didn't want to disappoint his master. Warren contemplated his subordinate's comment, albeit with a bit of that vampire superiority.

"Why?" Diego adjusted his glasses. "Did something happen?" His look had changed from charming prince to a twenty-something kid again.

"I'll take care of it." Warren faced me. "I don't expect there to be a next time. Diego will get you to your destination."

Then he turned and walked down the hall. I watched until his form disappeared.

"Ahem." Diego held out a puffy long coat, waiting for me to slip into it.

It was better than the slip of a gown I wore, and I'd take whatever I could get. Life had taught me to never pass up an offer.

Next, Diego offered shoes. "I sort of disposed of your clothing."

"Getting rid of any traces for plausible deniability?" Thank goodness, they hadn't shoved me into an incinerator.

A guilty grimace flashed over his expression. "Something like that."

I slipped into the name brand tennis shoes. They fit pretty good. "I'm keeping these." I kicked my foot back to look at my fashion statement. A long coat and athletic footwear. I only needed a pair of dark glasses to complete the whole ensemble.

"You look very Sophia Richie." Diego snapped his fingers with pizzazz.

Strutting my stuff back and forth like the long step was a catwalk, I pranced, careful to stay on the one step he'd told me to stay on.

Diego lifted a hand in offering.

I did not take his hand. "Can I leave this step now?"

Diego nodded. "Yes. I'll take you to the Rusty Teapot now that you have shoes and a coat."

"Great!" I smiled too wide for it to be genuine. I wanted to get out of here.

"Follow me." Diego turned down a corridor opposite the one he'd come from, and I rushed to get behind him.

After another sharp turn, a long hallway led to a single door. An alligator pit could be behind that other side for all I knew, but I followed Diego because I believed he didn't want to hurt me. Crazy as that sounded, something told me I was in safe hands. Though, it could be from whatever power he used on me before, I was sure this feeling came from my gut and not arbitrary whispers in my head.

He opened the door to a black emptiness. Cold drifts of freezing air blasted me back. "Whoa."

"I know, but it's the only portal I have for the Rusty Teapot." Diego kept the door open and lifted his hand.

Portal? Vampires have portals? Great. It was the perfect snatch and grab. "You first."

Diego blinked. "Do you want to go home or not?"

"Ahhh, that's not home or the Rusty Teapot."

"It takes considerable concentration to do this, Miles." He closed his eyes as if in prayer for patience.

"Then explain it." No way was I trusting him blindly.

"Every restaurant has a freezer."

"And freezer's have locks."

Diego wiggled his fingers. "I'm going in with you. I'll guide you."

I waited for my gut reaction, and no whispers came.

Demons didn't get a lot of trust. Go figure. Faith was a power of its own. Once a contract of faith was broken, the likelihood of extending trust again was nil. Demons knew that more than most. Relying on him put my confidence to the test. He was my only way home. Both he and Warren apologized. For that reason alone, I took his hand.

"Thank you," he mumbled in relief. He knew he'd messed up, and this was more trust than he deserved.

Diego guided me into the dark room and closed the door, where we plunged into frozen darkness.

CHAPTER 5

PANIC CLAWED AT MY throat.

"It's okay, Miles. I'll get us through." Diego squeezed my hand, the only warm part of me.

I shifted from foot to foot and closed the front of my coat. Diego's thoughtfulness of shoes and jacket proved he wasn't a complete monster. His forethought to spare me walking bare foot on freezing ground made me think better of him.

No, Miles. I shivered in the cold. This is what these monsters do. They treat you kindly to get your guard down, then strike.

Diego kept walking in the dark, taking me with him.

"Oh my God." I rubbed one arm trying to get warmth into my bones.

Metal clicked, a rusty hinge squeaked, and another door opened. He pulled me through into the light and let the heavy meat locker slam shut behind us.

The air was stifling hot after the tundra we walked through. Chefs worked over a grill, some brought tubs to counters, others chopped, another pulled out bread from an oven, but none of them noticed us walking out of the freezer. The smells increased, and I swallowed my hunger.

Diego hauled me through the kitchen with practiced ease. In no time, we were out on the restaurant floor of the Rusty Teapot, and he sat me in a booth and scooted in across from me.

The Rusty Teapot specialized in twenty-four-hour breakfast. That's all they did. The motif of the place was quaint country table linens, wood cutout chicken silhouettes, permeated by the smell of bacon and eggs. Plaques claiming "Home was where the breakfast was cooked" and "Get your sausage here" made the theme homey. From beignet to waffles, if it was breakfast, it was here, including any tea from around the world.

He interlaced his fingers and set his elbows on the table, his chin resting on top of his knuckles.

"You took that well."

I narrowed my eyes and brushed warmth into my skin. The cold didn't affect him. Anyone would be freezing, even with a coat. What the hell is this guy? Demon? Wizard? Witch? Vampire? Definitely not human.

"I've seen what demons can do," I murmured, settling on the best assumption. "Didn't know teleportation was one of them."

"Portal, not teleportation." He reached for his napkin and set it in his lap.

"No difference."

Diego huffed and rolled his eyes. "Yes, there is."

Dolores, the waitress on duty, set two menus down and took our drink order. Hot chocolate for me and water for Diego.

Getting home was great, but there was a problem with "portaling" here, and I couldn't help groan. "My car. It's out in the desert."

"Right." Diego stiffened. "I'll get you a new one."

"Diego..." I growled. "I want my car. You are not buying exclusivity with that when I already have perfectly good transportation."

He cast a serious gaze even as he lifted his hands to hide his mouth. "I could get you anything. You wouldn't have for want. I was serious when I offered anything in exchange for your"—he looked around—"talents."

My blood boiled. Diego went from disarming sidekick to egotistical henchmen.

"I'm not for sale." The half lie made my face burn. It was only a small truth because there was something I wanted. Information that would lead to my mother. No one knew of her. She was a nonentity. I'd tried finding her for years, to no avail, but the name, Eli Florentine, held power. Some avoided anything to do with him, some ignored me and walked away, but some would give me information about him. Since he was her confidant, he might know where she was. I could trade for the information to find him. Then I remembered Warren's reaction in the limo when I asked about the Florentine vampire. He'd screamed for Diego and turned into ash. Was I in too deep trying to find my mom?

"Are you quitting as a donor?" Diego's eyebrows rose.

I crossed my arms and said nothing.

Diego sighed. "You wanted to know something about someone."

That got my attention, and my breath snapped.

Compassion swirled deep within his eyes. He said nothing and waited me out. I decided instead to change the subject.

"You're not vampires." Because there was only one safe place for the undead. Sunlight. The sun filtered into the Rusty Teapot. Warren had stood in the soft hues of stained glass in front of a crucifix and on the steps before a huge window.

"No." Diego smirked and tilted his head.

"But you drink blood."

He scanned the restaurant then answered. "Warren does."

"And you?" I asked.

The ends of a coy smile reached beyond his hands, still hiding his mouth. "I don't want to scare you."

Oh, fucking hell. Not a blood drinker, but something else. What could be worse than a vampire?

Diego's mirth disappeared, and he slid his hands across the table. "Tell me about your mother."

My first inclination was to lean away even as whispers told me to trust him. "Stop that."

Diego pulled away, and the voices faded. "I just... thought we could trade."

"That trust ended when you catfished me, then left me to Warren."

Sighing, he knew he was in the wrong.

A familiar chime dinged from Diego's coat, and he pulled out a familiar hot pink Hello Kitty case.

My phone! "Hey! That's mine!"

Diego pushed it over the table, and I snatched it with a pout.

Five missed calls. All from Lilly. As if her twenty text messages weren't enough.

Sorry. Been out for a few days. I sent the text, and she replied back.

OMG. Are you okay????

Yes

Where u @

I looked over to Diego who calmly waited. He'd gone back to loveable goofball, but I knew underneath his veneer he was deadly. I debated whether or not to get her caught up in this.

w Diego. I set my phone down.

That was vague enough. Otherwise, she might come running.

"Miles?" His soft tone set off my alarm bells.

Food came. I hadn't ordered anything, but Diego didn't look surprised to see a giant plate of eggs, toast, fruit, bacon, and a blueberry muffin set down in front of me along with my hot chocolate.

"Ummm..." That was a lot of food.

"Thank you," Diego said to the waitress.

Dolores touched his shoulder, and I saw the faintest of shivers run through him. "You're welcome, hun. Anything else?"

"No." He shook his head and sipped his water.

When she left, I narrowed my eyes. "I didn't order."

"You didn't have to."

God, I was hungry. "How did you—"

"Eat." He gestured to the food. "You look like you're going to faint. And"—he looked away—"it's the least I can do."

"Yeah, it is." I tucked into the eggs first. Protein. "I'd say you own me about three-fifty per ounce." My forced acceptance of being drained deserved a heavy penalty fee.

"I was quoted half that." He smiled and took another sip of water.

"That's with the asshole fee." I shoved toast in my mouth and glared at him.

Diego snorted. "There's already money in your account. I'm sure you'll find it sufficient to cover your costs and for the ah... discretion of the buyer's identity."

"I didn't sign an NDA." I gobbled the rest of the eggs and started on the blueberry muffin. Truth be told, I wouldn't talk about selling my blood to anyone.

Like a demon, he pulled out a contract from nowhere—or maybe his ass—and dropped a two-page legal document. "Sign it, and I'll double what's in your bank account." He watched me. The mask of innocence and naivety settled well onto his face.

Checking my phone bank app, I stopped eating, then coughed. A lot of zero's accompanied the number at the end of my balance. Twenty-five thousand might not seem like a lot to other people, but for a half-serious orphaned college student looking for her mother and having to take care of herself, it was enough to cover rent, tuition, private investigator fees, and groceries for many months. For the first time in my life, I wouldn't have to pay late charges for one thing or another. It could make a girl cry.

"Ummm..." If I was evil, I could say that maybe Warren's identity was worth more. But I didn't know him from any other Balrog, so I shrugged my shoulders. "Okay. I won't tell."

He pulled out a pen and held it out.

"I'm not signing that thing. Are you crazy? You're a demon." For all I knew, I'd sign my life blood away.

"It will be worth your while if you do."

Tempting offer.

"Please?" He lifted the pen. "For my sanity sake?"

Like he had any or deserved it. I scanned the document to make sure there weren't clauses claiming my blood belonged to Warren until I died. After a long look, I snatched the pen and signed at the dotted line. Though, it did make me curious if I was leaving money on the table.

"Thank you," he sighed.

"But I still want my car back."

My cell dinged. Another message from Lilly. b there

Great. She was coming over. Ugh. That girl had me on radar.

its okay I got this

But no matter what I said, Lilly did whatever she wanted.

Diego got up and slapped a bill down on the table. "You sure? I can get you a new car."

"I'm sure. I want my car." Demons are generous in their own way, but if I accepted his offer, it might be that the pink slip was in his name, and he could claim it stolen anytime.

I started in on another bite of toast not willing to leave. Diego was right. I was hungry.

"Very well, then. I'll have it returned here in an hour. Maybe less."

Ha. Very funny. Driving to the desert and back would take him half a day, but his face remained serious. After the portal thing, I'd have to admit he might have the capability to do what he said. Like magic, he pulled out a key ring.

Not any set but my key ring. Diego unclipped the Honda fob, then handed over the rest of my keys.

A stream of anger started filtering insults in my head, but he had considered me dead. I guess I should be thankful that he hadn't gotten rid of my car in order to hide my murder.

"Goodbye, Miles." He said it like he hoped it to be the last we ever saw of each other.

"Wait..." He was leaving too soon, and fury gave me the courage to ask for any information I could about my mother's whereabouts. "If you find anything about Eli Florentine, anything at all, please, tell me?"

He stared off and drew his eyebrows together.

When he didn't say anything, I added, "It would be worth—a lot to me." Knowing anything was worth being drained again.

"Okay." He took off his glasses and washed his face with a hand.

"Thank you."

Diego left the same way we had come, texting on his phone as he went, through the kitchen. No shouts of indignant chefs or any blip of acknowledgment he'd gone through an employee-only area erupted. Somehow, I doubted I could walk into their freezer and come out another side much less walk unnoticed through the kitchen.

I finished my food fast as a racehorse over the finish line and spied the single greenback he'd left. It was a crisp hundred-dollar bill. Interesting.

"There you are." Lilly's melodic voice drifted from the other side of the table. She sat across from me in the booth. "Where have you been?"

"With a client." I straightened and boasted. I was at least twenty-five thousand dollars richer. Which also reminded me that I owed some of it to a certain private investigator.

Her bright-blue eyes softened. "Mixing pleasure with business?"

"No." I took a sip of my cooling hot chocolate.

She straightened. "Anything about your mom?"

At that I sighed. "No."

Lilly didn't know everything, but she took my campaign to find Pepper, my mother, seriously. For that, she was a good friend.

"Has Eustachys gotten back to you?"

Aliprand Eustachys was the private investigator I'd found through my hard work being a donor. I'd gotten his number after asking too many questions from a vampire wannabe that didn't have money but did have connections. Eustachys had a knack for the paranormal and hadn't given pause when I said the Florentine name. He'd asked me to specify. Dropping the term enclave did give him pause. Then he charged me double for his services.

Scrolling through messages I did in fact get an unexpected message from Eustachys saying to come in. Probably so I could pay him.

"Yeah," I said. Though the text was sent two days ago.

My fingers danced over the keyboard on my phone as I responded.

be there this afternoon.

It was always good to let him know I'd be at his office because I never caught him there unless I had an appointment.

"Sooo…" Lilly drawled out the question she was dying to ask. "How did it go with Diego?"

I shot her a steely glare. "Guess I can't complain." I was still alive and flush with money.

She rolled her eyes and let out an exasperated gasp. "I was hoping maybe you'd find something or at least get a boyfriend."

Um. No. I didn't have time to ask between being kidnapped, fighting a demon, dying, and being pulled through a freaking worm hole. "Um, he didn't know anything."

Lilly scoffed with audible disgust. "All my efforts were for nothing?"

"I wouldn't say that." Heat crept up my cheeks.

"Oh?" She leaned forward, interested in the things I hadn't said. "Did you perhaps—"

"No!" The flush radiated through my entire face. "We didn't do that."

"Why not?" Lilly smiled with predatory mirth. "Sex isn't a crime, ya know."

"Oh my God, Lilly." I didn't have time for that. "Just… it was okay. He took a lot out of me, that's all."

She looked worried instead of placated, but I was done with her questions.

"I'm tired. I'm going to my one class, then sleep, then I'll see Eustachys."

Lilly folded her hands, entwining her fingers, her voice low and laced with a hint of danger in her question. "Did he hurt you?"

I stared into cold, hard eyes. Fury swirled behind Lilly's mask of calm. I reached out to her and tried to use the comfort of touch to express my gratitude that someone gave a damn. Before I could reach her, she pulled away and directed an angry glare at me. "Answer the question."

A slow, suffering sigh flushed through my nose. It made me realize I didn't know much about Lilly. She was a mystery. I knew I shouldn't have reached for her. She had something in her past she couldn't let go of. Something bad. Something that made her shy away from touch. "Life is pain, Lilly. But it means you're alive."

Her smile came slow as the dawn and beautiful as a sunset. She traced a delicate finger along her jaw line. "You remind me so much of myself when I was younger."

I snorted. "What are you, sunny side down from twenty?"

She laughed. "Ditch class. Go rest."

Her expression turned back into a scowl as she looked toward the kitchen. Right where Diego left.

"What are you thinking?" I asked.

"That I should give Diego etiquette lessons."

"Don't." I let out a breath. "He was fine. It was fine. Don't make a big deal out of it."

She tossed her long red hair. "Okay, but only because you asked."

A part of me liked the idea of Lilly giving Diego shit for what he had done, but that would lead her into the path of Warren. That I would protect her from. "I'm serious. He paid me well for my time. Drop it."

She shrugged. "Fine. I can get back at him in other ways."

"What other ways?"

"I don't have to introduce him to donors." She was still nonchalant, but her suggestion might be the better solution.

"That would work."

Lilly smiled again, and this time, it held no nefarious double entendre. "Nighty night." She stood, waved a kiss to me, and flowed out of the restaurant like an evil debutant ready to set the world on fire. She was the type with something to do and places to be. I wished I could be more like her.

CHAPTER 6

WHEN I REGISTERED FOR school, I'd had a genius moment and took classes Tuesday through Thursday so I could do research and homework on Friday. I'd planned to sell my blood for rent, tuition, food, and finding my mom Friday and Saturday night, leaving me to recover Sunday and Monday. That was my best laid plan that didn't always go as scheduled.

My Tuesday morning class started at ten. That gave me three hours to change and find a ride. I texted my Tuesday appointment, Scott Theodosius, and jumped into the shower. Hot water hit my skin, washing three days of grime down the drain. I grabbed my loofa and soaped up. Familiarity let me sink into past events.

Nobody knew my mother. Asking for her was like looking for a needle in a haystack and the needle not even being in the haystack. She was a nonentity, just like I'd been until I'd been put in the system. That had been a nightmare. Getting paperwork on a child that hadn't been born, in the eyes of society, was like being a ghost. On paper, I was Makayla Evans. My real name was Chamomile

Eirian. Two feet in two different worlds with only paper holding them apart.

I rubbed my neck, making sure any dried blood went with the grit of days without a shower and found smooth skin. Vampires leave shiny scars when they bite, but the mutilations inflicted by humans pretending to be vampires are worse. My neck was covered in lumps and marks that made me invest in turtlenecks and scarves. Was being the operative word. I didn't feel the awful blemishes on my neck, but felt smooth, sensitive skin. I had to see, just to check the blemishes were gone and stepped out of the shower to my bathroom mirror.

Same as I'd felt, my neck was flawless. My gasping sob surprised me. I'd accepted the imperfection as life. I'd buried the disappointment of a constant ugly reminder of my "uniqueness." Tears leaked unbidden and rolled down my cheeks. This was a gift.

"Thank you." I closed my eyes and put a hand over my heart. My core swirled in gratefulness, and warmth grew in my chest.

If I had his phone number, I'd call Warren to give him my gratitude, but paying it forward would have to do.

My phone dinged, and I saw that Scott answered my plea for a ride, killing two birds with one stone. I could give him my blood and make it to my class. As luck would have it, Scott was not a neck biter. He said he wanted blood for medical reasons. I suspected he had lupus as some sufferers felt better having a shot of healthy blood occasionally. Thus, my fresh neck didn't have to be marred again too soon.

I had a little over an hour before he got here, so I finished my shower and started getting ready for the day.

I knew Scott, so my no-private-places rule didn't apply. Plus, I needed a ride.

An hour later, I heard a thump on my door and checked the peephole. I saw hair. Specifically, short wiry, curly black hair. Most likely Scott but better safe than sorry.

"Hello?"

A muffled slurring eked out. "Here at your command, Liebling."

Definitely Scott. I opened the door, and a five-foot-ten man nearly tumbled inside, but he kept his balance with the help of the doorway molding. Even almost falling into my apartment, he still looked half asleep.

"Oh, wow, you really aren't a morning person."

"Mmm..." He swayed in the hall and groaned. His tight black pants might actually be helping him to stay on his feet, but his swimmer's build and combat boots were probably more of a help keeping him upright than his eclectic clothing style.

His chin had a bit of stubble, and his hair was jet-black and tousled enough to make me think I'd dragged him out of bed with my request.

In a ragged voice, he said, "It's so early."

I snorted. "Nine in the morning is early?"

One eye peeked open, and a playful smirk lit up his face. "Noon is my daybreak."

"We have the same class." He never missed one of Professor Nightshade's sessions every Tuesday at 10 a.m. To be fair, he always looked wrecked during our lectures.

"Ungh." His single open eye closed again. "Invite me in."

I stared at his lean, athletic build. Pale skin, hair like crow's feathers, thick eyebrows, prominent cheekbones, and strong stubble-lined jaw presented a handsome face without standing out. Stylish Scott was not just a client but also a loyal friend, but my heart was shaken, and my confidence shot. It's not paranoia when they genuinely are after you.

"How about you prove you're human and step through the door yourself." I pulled back and held the door. If he was a vampire, he wouldn't be able to cross the threshold without my permission.

Scott stopped swaying and went stock still. Both eyes slowly opened, and his striking hazel orbs reflected concern. He blinked a few times, and his stare zeroed in on my neck. He said nothing, but there was concern mixed in with mindful calculation in the flecks of gold speckling among his irises.

Then, he smiled best as any night owl awoken too early could, lifted his leg up like a Turkish soldier, and leaned forward. His boot slapped down on the other side of my threshold, and he slid himself all the way into my apartment.

"Damn, my mystique is ruined," he said. "Don't tell the others."

"Your secret's safe with me." I put a hand over my heart. "Come on, I know what will get you awake." I headed to my kitchen.

"Hey, now I have a girlfriend." He smiled, one eye barely cracked open.

"Oh? Is she in the circle?" Referring to our group of wannabe vampires as a coven or an enclave didn't sit well with me.

"I'm teaching her our ways. I was going to introduce you to her tonight." He followed me into my single-room apartment. On the right, I'd folded up my Murphy bed to leave a clean, open space making a path to the bathroom hallway that led to the shower, sink, and closet. To the left was the full kitchen bar. Two stools stood on the outside of the alcove. I offered Scott one, and when he was seated, I went to my fridge, got a prepacked shot size blood bag, and put it in the microwave for seventeen seconds.

"Ughngh." Scott slumped over my kitchen top.

"Will you be joining the living anytime soon?" I teased, but I'd never seen him this way. The ever-effusive Scott Theodosius always bounced around with energy in spades whenever I saw him, but I'd always talked to him at night.

"Gimme a minute," Scott said in a muffled huff, rolling his forehead on the kitchen counter.

We had time before class, so I grabbed water from the fridge and uncapped the top. I set one bottle down for him and downed my own.

When the microwave dinged, I cut open the bag, poured it in a shot glass, and slid it over to him. He eyed the blood and hung his head over the glass. Then he downed the shot.

"So, what's your girlfriend's name?" I cleaned the counter as I watched Scott go from sleep deprived to effervescent.

He told me everything there was to know about Tika in the time it took walking from my apartment, driving to school, all the way into class. That boy was stuck on her. He told me everything from her shoe size, six, to the feel of her long auburn hair. For anyone who liked redheads, he painted her like the perfect full-figured, blue-eyed ginger beauty.

Professor Rowan Nightshade, who furiously scribbled on papers at his desk when we walked in, was also a redhead, graced with more strawberry than blond hair, with fair skin and green eyes. The forensic case studies teacher looked like a grown-up Sherman, Peabody's counterpart, that had gained a little bit of muscle.

Scott and I sat together. I pulled out my notes, and Scott pulled out a recorder.

This was the only class I paid any mind. Chemistry, biology, even criminal procedure were all great, but this was the class I felt could help me find my mom. I never missed it.

I felt a presence, and Lilly was there beside me, in the opposite seat from Scott.

"Hey." I smiled.

"I knew you'd come." She nodded and leaned in her chair, relaxed and focused on our professor. No notebook, no pen, no recorder. It made me curious, and now that we knew each other, I had the nerve to ask how she could keep up with her studies.

"How do you remember everything?"

Those electric blue eyes flashed, and she smiled. "I have an eidetic memory. I can also recall conversations. Besides, remembering a cutie like Professor Rowan Nightshade is easy."

"Lucky." The only images I had perfect recall for were the horrors from my early life.

Finally, enough students came in for the professor to stop scribbling. Adjusting his glasses, he stood up.

Our amphitheater classroom made every seat a perfect view of the board which had in dry-erase marker "Case 23-0404-Lightning."

Professor Nightshade addressed us. "Good morning, everyone. Today, we're delving into an unusual case that has baffled both forensic experts and meteorologists alike."

Our forensic professor always brought the most unusual cases, which was one reason I never missed his class. Last week, he'd shown us a victim with telltale signs of a very familiar circumstance—the happy jitteriness of someone winning the lottery. Of course, I couldn't jump out and say, "Vampire's did it!" But our prof had a certain glint in his eye that made me both wary and hopeful. I'd considered approaching him about helping me, but as young and innocent as he looked, there was something that made me cautious. In the end, I kept my mouth shut.

"Three victims," Professor Nightshade continued. "All struck by lightning in the same park, on the same day."

Wow. What were the odds?

Lilly leaned forward, her hand shooting up. "Professor," she purred. "I read somewhere that being struck by lightning is over a million to one chance. Any idea how three people could be hit at the same time in the same location?"

At first, the professor's face froze, like he hadn't expected anyone to know the odds. Then his smile beamed. "Exactly! Isn't it fascinating? Statistically, it's almost impossible. Yet that's the situation." He spread his hands wide. "When we first investigated the case, it raised a host of questions. Was it mere coincidence, or could there be something more sinister at play?"

That gave me pause. He was giving us the most unusual study examples.

"What do you mean by 'sinister'? Surely it was a freak accident?" Lilly said with effusive sarcasm.

"You seem familiar with the case," the professor said.

"Because I am." Lilly didn't expand on why.

The professor nodded like it was normal for someone to know about such a weird case. "A freak accident. That's one theory, certainly." The professor straightened his glasses. "However, when we examined the details surrounding the victims—two men and a woman—we began to uncover connections that suggested they might have been targeted."

Scott huffed. "How is that possible?"

"Indeed." Our professor picked up a stack of folders. "I know this is old-school, but here are copies of the case files, compliments of Officer Corey." He gave the pile of folders to one of the students, who took one and passed around the rest.

"Take a minute to look over the papers." Professor Nightshade went back to his desk and scribbled on his notebook.

The report indicated that all three had connections to a controversial environmental protest occurring in the park that day. I thought it possible that someone wanted to send a message to the protestors.

"So, Professor?" I said, and he looked up. "Do you think the lightning could've been a kind of cover-up?"

"Yeah," Scott chimed in. "But wouldn't that be impossible?"

"Or maybe"—Professor Nightshade smiled with that knowing twinkle in his eye, like Peabody when he was explaining history or science—"it would draw attention away from foul play. Three people being struck by lightning in a public space. Could be the perfect cover for something else."

Lilly hadn't even opened her folder and kept her eyes on the professor. "The distraction could lead to other incidents going unnoticed. Did you find anything in the investigation that supported the idea of foul play?"

Wow. Lilly was so cool. She sounded like an investigator.

"Yes." Professor Nightshade fiddled with his green bow tie and adjusted his glasses several times. "We dug deeper into the victims' backgrounds. The woman was an activist who had received multiple threats leading up to the protest."

"It says here one of the men had recently withdrawn significant sums of money," Scott said. "Larger than anyone could account for in their personal finances."

"Oh." How suspicious. "That creates a picture."

Lilly nodded and smiled at me. "If someone had it out for these individuals, how do you connect the dots?"

Our prof became animated, using his hands for emphasis, and said, "This is where forensics shines. We utilized elements like digital forensics, analyzing social media interactions, and reviewing CCTV footage from the park. While we couldn't pinpoint who set everything in motion, we started to identify individuals tied to the threats against the victims."

Reviewing the documents and the conversations leading down this path, I could see where the lightning strikes could throw a rational mind off. Normal people hadn't seen what I had in my short lifetime. While others might focus on how this happened, I pushed the extraordinary circumstance to the side. "So, it wasn't just about the lightning itself but rather the environment surrounding the event that led to their tragic fate?"

Professor Nightshade smiled. "Exactly. The forensic analysis looked at both physical evidence and social contexts. Ultimately, the case challenged our preconceived notions about accidents versus intentional harm. Sometimes, the most sinister motives are hidden in plain sight, aren't they?"

Lilly smirked. "And to think it all started with a mystery of lightning strikes. It's incredible how many angles we can explore with forensics."

"Precisely!" Professor Nightshade said. "Let's remember that every case comes down to details—no matter how bizarre they may seem. Now, break into groups and come up with your own theories about this case using the forensic methods we've discussed. I want a five-page report, double spaced. Please don't make me format your files. It's due by Friday, midnight."

Lilly, Scott, and I teamed up, while Professor Nightshade, with his hands in his vest pockets, looked satisfied at his students.

Curiosity got the better of me, and I turned to huddle with my group. "Was it lightning that killed them?"

Lilly nodded. "Sure was."

Scott raised his eyebrows. "This has got to be made up."

Lilly stuck her head closer to Scott and teased, "If I told you some vampires can control the weather and call down lightening, then what would you say?"

He thought about it, bobbing his head. "Okay, I'm in. You think a vampire did it?"

She chuckled. "I didn't say that."

"What can control lightning?" I asked.

Lilly started ticking off her fingers. "Witches, vampires, Thor, Zeus, a hammerkop."

"A what?"

"Hammerkop," Lilly repeated louder. "You know, a thunderbird."

Professor Nightshade called out, "Try to stay in the realm of science, please, not myths."

I heard a titter from a nearby group.

"Right." Scott nodded. "Find the why. Don't get stuck on the how."

"So." I put forth a theory. "Guy A draws out money. Maybe he wants to pay Guy B who's a hit man, for Girl C. It goes haywire, and everyone involved gets killed."

"How very, everyone dies." Lilly pulled back.

Scott leaned his chin in his hand with a pensive thoughtfulness. "No happy ending for anyone?"

"Isn't that life?" I shrugged.

"Agreed." Lilly nodded.

Scott kept his mouth shut and shook his head.

"Bah!" I waved my hand. "This guy's dating the girl of his dreams. Everything looks rosy to him right now."

Lilly rolled her eyes. "Fool."

"Anyway..." Scott's ears were bright red. "That doesn't explain the why."

"Revenge," Lilly supplied.

"Or love," I said.

We theorized until I started falling asleep with my eyes open. Scott had enough time to drop me off at home before his next class. I needed to start on Nightshade's paper and take a nap before I saw Eustachys, the PI investigating to find my mother.

CHAPTER 7

SCOTT DROPPED ME OFF at the Rusty Teapot. My car was nowhere in sight. Though, parking in this neighborhood was challenging. I hoped Diego was treating my little Honda well.

The entrance to my apartment wasn't in the restaurant, so I walked to the alleyway behind the building. Around the street corner, inlaid within the brick walls, was a narrow corridor of stairs. So narrow that I remembered the trouble it was to have the burly delivery guys squeeze through it carrying my bed into my large eight-hundred-square-foot studio.

I ascended into the main hall—where six doors lined in rows of three on each side—and pulled out my keys. My room was the last door on the left. I'd never met my neighbors, and in fact, I didn't know if I even had neighbors. The place was always so quiet.

Today, though, I wasn't alone.

Thomas, the first guy I'd met at the rave, stood in front of the door across from mine, key in hand. Panic clutched my heart.

"Ms. Evans!" Thomas—the person that got a lot right, the person I'd vote most likely to be a vampire pretending to be human acting like a wannabe vampire—stood feet from me. His teeth piercing white. Before my eyes, his incisors elongated into a double-toothed smile.

I had no doubt now. Thomas was a vampire.

Caught off guard, my body reacted on a visceral level, and I backed up—right off the steps. My stomach lurched as I started to fall.

"Miles!" Thomas dashed, reaching me faster than the blink of an eye. He caught me, pulled us from the stairs, and pushed my back against the wall.

Fudge. I'd been on the run so long that all my vampire social graces were pushed to the wayside, abandoning all reason and trying for a getaway. Not good. Stirring up a vampire's instinct was never advisable.

Two arms jailed me in place as Thomas loomed over me in the hallway of my apartment. He smelled of expensive suit, soap, and nothing else. He didn't have a signature scent that was strictly his. He didn't breathe. The fast response effortless.

"Don't move," his voice rasped.

The way he said it, with breathy effort, twisted my insides. Vampires were predators. Blood dolls were prey. I might as well have screamed, Chase me, catch me, eat me. People did not outrun a vampire. I'd tried and triggered his other instincts far different from a human.

I stood frozen with my back against the wall, fighting my own instincts that would only get my blood drained. My heart pounded. It must have sounded as loud as thunder to him.

Thomas didn't have his fake vampire regalia. He wore a navy suit and slacks with a complimentary blue shirt contrasting a white tie. His iris pooled over like blood. This time they weren't contacts. He closed his eyes and combed his fingers through his short blond hair, straightening the wild locks. Canine teeth pinched his lower lip.

"Thank you," he said, but he still hadn't opened his eyes.

His nose flared, and taking a breath in, he moaned. His body quivered. His hands held him up. Was it to keep me from escaping or to keep a safe distance so he wouldn't sink his teeth into me?

Yeah, yeah. I smelled good—maybe different than a human but tasty to a bloodsucker. He had the sense not to mention it though.

"How... how are you?" He still hadn't opened his eyes.

"I'd be a lot better if I wasn't pinned to a wall." The rollercoaster in my stomach climbed another hill and waited for the fall.

Thomas smirked with his eyes closed, but his face looked strained. He was having a hard time controlling himself. My mouth tasted like iron.

I needed to gauge how much I was screwed. "Open your eyes."

Solid black pupils overtook his blue iris's, absorbing the light until twin holes of nothingness shifted, then he turned his head to the side, and pointed his gaze away from me.

Crap. He was too far gone. My bladder became heavy. Maybe the smell of ammonia would deter him. Or maybe it would mingle with the scent of my fear.

"Look at me," I ground out.

"Miles—"

"I know what you are." The scent of fear, heavy and thick, wafted between us. "I'd rather see it coming." Perfect, I was going to get drained twice this week.

Thomas snapped his head to me, his eyes blown out and feral. "If you know, then get your heartbeat under one-twenty."

"Don't growl at me." I put on my brave face, but the cloying monster of anemia clawed its way forward, making everything spin.

Shock, then amusement colored his face. He leaned away, but not far enough to let me out from his cage of arms.

Every part of my body betrayed my superficially inward calm, revealing my true state of mind. Sweat beading my forehead, I stood with my hands balled at my sides, and ground out, "What are you doing here anyway?"

For a response, I got a soft, dreamy stare and a "Mmm... I live here."

"What? Since when?" Keep the vampire talking so he can get a grip on himself. Give him time to shake out of his blood trance—a state of euphoria, where the vampire felt safe enough to enjoy the smells, and sensations, before striking like a viper. It was comparatively like that moment of hunger, where the smells of the finely cooked meal made one's mouth water, but waiting to dig in, respecting the host who prepared the food.

"I moved last week." He traced a finger along my neck, fixated on my pulse.

His touch made me feel naked. My heart rate wasn't slowing down. He remained in his blood trance. This was my chance.

Thomas was a vampire. A real one. He'd convinced me he wasn't a bloodsucker at the rave by having enough "off" to persuade me he might be human. Throwing in enough expectation about what vampires were, he tossed off the scent of anyone who knew what to look for. He blended into humanity. Those types of vampires walked the line between worlds. He would know where I could find Eli, thus my mother.

"Such soft skin," he mumbled, caressing my throat.

"I... offer... a trade." My voice wobbling at the words. So much could go wrong.

Thomas brightened and pushed his leg between mine, took hold of my thigh, and pressed against my body.

Smart man. He wouldn't allow me to get in a jab to the nuts.

"I'm listening."

"I'm looking for someone."

He buried his nose in the crook of my neck. It felt intimate and wrong. I was vulnerable and not in a good way. I was making a deal with the devil without anything to back up my own safety. Like trying to make fair trade with a tiger in its own den, and without a gun for protection.

"You want information? Or do you want help looking for them?"

He wasn't totally out of control if he were thinking on his feet. Before I could answer, an inhuman growl rattled the doors. The floor rumbled. Large fingers wrapped around Thomas's throat, and then he was ripped away.

Warren—huge, threatening, and very angry—twisted Thomas around and pushed him backward to the stairs.

Thomas teetered at the edge of the top step, arms at his sides, face pale, the only thing keeping him from falling was Warren gripping the ends of Thomas's white tie.

One of the things I knew about demons was they didn't have an innate fear of falling. Thus, Thomas didn't flail as he tipped further back. His arms remained at his side. It was the little things that tipped off vampires. This was one of them.

Now that he was occupied, I didn't waste any time. I ran for my door and scrambled with my house key. The teeth scraped against the lock as I jiggled the handle.

"Mine!" Warren growled.

Great. Just great. Like I said, there's always a catch. Demons never let a blood doll go. I was territory.

Stark fear loomed in Thomas's eyes. "I have not claimed her."

Finally, my key slammed home, and I twisted the lock. The door opened, and I stepped over the threshold. The legend about demons not entering a home unless invited was sort of true. Enough that I felt safe to keep the door open and watch.

"You're young." Warren looked Thomas up and down.

My new neighbor scoffed. "Compared to you, everyone is young." His body leaned beyond the point of no return. If Warren let go of his tie, Thomas would tumble down the stairs.

"Do you not have an enclave?" Warren let the tie slip an inch through his fingers before tightening his hold. Just enough for the threat to sink in.

Thomas dug his fingers at the base of his neck trying to hold on to his noose. It was the only indication he was uncomfortable.

"Wait…" I said. My body trembled. I couldn't explain it other than human compassion. Or madness. It was probably madness, but as one who'd been through and seen enough suffering, I didn't have tolerance for watching more. "Let him go."

Warren turned his red-gold eyes toward me. Then he opened his hand, and the vampire tumbled. Thomas cursed as I heard him crash down the stairs.

Oh, heck. Warren had taken me literally.

"What are you doing?" My first instinct was to run, help Thomas, but I stood behind the threshold.

"Letting him go." Warren cocked his head, looking me up and down. His nose flared and the look on his face was nearly comical. A glimmer of anger masked his usually calm tone.

"You're worried for him?" He took an aggressive step forward. "You're worried for him and afraid of me? Yet you were terrified enough to—" He broke off. "Fine. I'll leave."

"No. Wait!" Was I out of my mind? Apparently. "I'm… thank… I…" God. Everything out of my mouth was going to get me in trouble. Warren was a blood-drinking demon, but I wasn't sure if he was a vampire. Thanking him could mean the same to him as saying, "I'm now your indentured servant." Saying I was grateful might make him think I owed him a favor. Any kind of gratitude would mean he'd have the advantage.

He studied me. That same dour face and taut shoulders gave him a tense air, as if he was always holding something back.

"You are welcome?" His eyebrows lifted, and the vulnerable innocence conflicted against his actions.

"Blasted hell!" Thomas yelled up the stairs. "I live here!"

Warren slid his gaze around the place. "My condolences."

"Hey!" I crossed my arms. The place wasn't that bad.

Warren stepped my way, expectant.

I grabbed the door and blocked his path with my body. "I don't owe either of you anything." Would I never learn to stop shooting off my mouth?

"Ah..." The right corner of Warren's mouth lifted in a cocksure half smile. "Treat me as you would a human. I won't extract favors or double meaning with your words."

"Says the blood hog that couldn't even hold back," I snorted, making light of it. But a twinge of pain twisted my heart. Fear. Dying was not less painful for me because I could resurrect myself.

A memory—a flash of his speed. The scene in the limo came back, and he was sitting across from me and then he was attached to my neck in half a blink.

My heart sped up. The upward winding of anxiety made it harder to breathe. I wanted to shut the door, but sudden movement and vampires didn't always go well. Don't run.

Warren snapped his hand over his chest, pressing against his heart—assuming he had one. "I am... sorry... for the pain I caused you. I regret it in more ways than one."

Thomas came running up the steps three at a time. "Leave her alone."

Oh fantastic. Nothing like two undead white knights fighting for my honor. "Look, I don't belong to either of you, so stop the macho posturing."

The two stared at each other ignoring my words.

"You would die, fledgling," Warren growled.

Thomas gave it right back. "It would be worth it to give Miles a chance to run from you."

Exasperated at their antics, I bemoaned, "As if you didn't pin me to the wall two minutes ago."

"I'm sorry." Thomas blanched, and his gaze flickered my way. "You surprised me." His face turned sour as he faced Warren, but his words addressed me. "I didn't expect to see you so soon after the other night."

Warren's nose flared, and the red-gold glow of his eyes intensified.

"And you"—I pointed to Warren—"are you following me?"

The demon stared at me like I was crazy and thinned his lips. Like he wanted to say something but didn't want to in front of company.

"I was pulled from a meeting. I should go." That was not what he was going to say, I could tell, but he stared at me as if he was asking permission to stay.

"Okay." I stood, not knowing if I could close the door or if that would trigger some demon instinct. They were weird like that. "Not like I asked you to come here."

He opened his mouth, then closed it. Warren cocked his head, parting his lips, again sucking in the air, tasting it.

Some kind of weird vibe was going on. He seemed reluctant to leave. I seemed reluctant to shut the door. His eyes assessed me, yet his attention would turn inward sometimes, then give me a considering glance. "Are you leaving?"

"Not now."

Warren eyed me. He might have been wondering why I kept the door open. "When you decide to leave, alert me. I'll escort you."

What the heck? "Not necessary."

Thomas snorted, gaining Warren's attention.

"Get out!" Warren hissed at his adversary.

"How dare you." The other vampire looked ready for murder.

They glared at each other until Thomas's full body started shaking. Whatever battle they were waging took its toll on Thomas. He spun to the apartment across the hall, opened the door, and slammed it behind him.

Alone with the Balrog, again. Fantastic.

"Are you well?" Warren asked.

"Just peachy."

He gave a curt nod of his chin and, by some miracle, climbed down the stairs without another word.

"Wait!" Oh crap... I might as well ask. Fortune favors the bold.

He stopped on a step, and his shoulders lifted and dropped on a sigh. Warren pivoted on the stairs and came back. His feet fell heavy on the floor. My heart dropped in apprehension, and he stopped abruptly with one step back.

I breathed in relief. He could reach me before I could shut the door, but the space between us gave me comfort.

Warren waited, not pressuring me to talk, and cast his eyes at everything except me.

"Do you remember what I asked for in trade when we first met?" I bit my nail, hoping he wouldn't have the same reaction as when I'd asked about Eli Florentine the first time.

He narrowed his eyes, getting straight to the point. "What do you want with him?"

"I want to find him."

"No."

The finality took my breath away. "Please?"

He pressed a hand to his heart. "Miles, I'm protecting you. Don't seek him out."

"Protecting me?" I scoffed. "You're not very good at it."

He winced and backed up like I'd struck him with a physical blow. We stared at each other for a ragged, worn minute before he turned around and walked down the stairs.

When I couldn't hear his footsteps anymore, I closed the door and breathed a sigh of relief. He was gone. No answers but disaster avoided. The tension lifted as I locked my door and turned to my living space.

Warren wouldn't give me any answers, but... Thomas. He was a vampire. I could ask Thomas the whereabouts of Eli Florentine. He might know, and I could trade for the information. But before I went and did that, I had to gather my wits about me. I had time. Thomas lived here, so I could at least compose myself so when I faced a vampire I wouldn't pee my pants.

My apartment was a large open studio. It was enough for a Murphy bed, a nightstand, and a study desk, the surface of which was covered in textbooks Professor Nightshade made required reading. My kitchenette stretched linear against the opposite wall of my bed. The best part of the place was the sliding doors leading to a small porch overlooking the street. This was living the dorm dream. No roommates. No curfew. No nosy neighbors.

A knock at the door came, and I shuffled over and looked out the peephole.

Scratch the nosy neighbor's part.

On the other side of the door, Thomas leaned against the stairway railing in front of my apartment.

My groan of frustration could be heard through the thin wood barrier.

"Miles... are you afraid of me now?" the whisper barely audible. "I wanted to apologize. And to make sure you're truly okay."

Vampires were susceptible to certain magic. One of them being love. Love of a home. Love of a person. Not the type of possessiveness or lust but the real stuff. It's why they couldn't trespass and watch people sleep or why they were careful with their prey. They had some weird paralysis around love.

So, while I hadn't lived here long, I could say with confidence that I loved this place. It was with this certainty that I could open the door and stand in my home without worrying that Thomas would enter.

He straightened and clasped his hands behind him. Throat bobbing and blue eyes pleading, he tossed a hurt smile.

"Yes, I'm okay," I said.

Thomas fidgeted and put his hands into his pockets as if not knowing what to do with his limbs. His actions screamed introvert.

"Good." He bobbed his head. "That's good. Ummm... so, I am sorry, honestly. I didn't want you to think I didn't have control... or anything."

"I thought you liked scaring people."

He deflated, but I wasn't buying his "poor me, I'm so helpless" shtick. To his credit, he did try to warn me away from Diego.

"That's not the true me. That's what people expect." He ran his fingers through his blond hair.

"Well, you do a good job of it." I turned the knob. "You've apologized. Just don't do it again." I went to close the door.

"Wait!" He reached out, then pulled back.

I lifted an eyebrow, ready to take that nap I promised myself.

"It's... you're not exclusive, or anything, right?" He bit his lip and looked around as if someone would pop out and ease drop on our conversation. "You're still freelancing?" The intensity in his eyes gave him away.

A blood doll with a vampire neighbor willing to pay. The money could be convenient, but the scenario could also get complicated, though. I never stayed in one place for very long, always searching for the Florentine Enclave.

"Maybe," I said.

He smiled in relief. "At least it's not an outright no."

I snorted. "As if 'no' ever stopped a vampire."

Thomas went serious. "It's an acceptable answer."

"Well, I'll be. A consensual vampire."

"You said something about a trade?" The hopeful lilt to his voice brought back the matter at hand. My mom.

"I did." Despite his efforts at keeping things light, instinctual hesitation clogged my throat.

Thomas swaggered forward using the prowess of his attractiveness as a means of disarming my reluctance. As a man, minus his contact lenses and vampire alter ego, Thomas was alluring. Blond, blue-eyed, tan skin, Scandinavian features, tall—not overly so like Warren—presented him as boyfriend material. Any coed would snap him up even with his penchant for blood. In my circles, maybe because of it, even.

His sexy saunter inched him closer to my door. "What did you have in mind?"

Thomas reached out to lean against my doorframe going for the iconic bad-boy look. When his hand touched wood, a loud crack and a spark sent him reeling back.

"Fuck!" He shook his hand out. "Mother... puss bucket... how long have you lived here?"

I smirked and relaxed against my hall. "A few months."

"And you live alone?" Thomas rubbed at his hurt hand.

"Getting a bit personal, eh?" Was he trying to gauge my threshold?

He held his hands up in supplication. "That is one heck of a shield is all."

"Thanks." I was going to take my instincts' advice and sleep before making any agreements. I was punch-drunk tired. "Hey look, can we discuss this later?"

"Yeah, sure." He looked annoyed, and I couldn't blame him though it was his own fault. "I wanted to see if you were okay."

"I am. Thanks." I didn't have the same compulsion to be careful with my words around Thomas as I did with Warren. Thomas was a vampire. Those demons I understood, but there was something different about Warren.

Thomas waved goodbye, and I closed my door. Time for some shut eye. Even if I'd technically been asleep for three days, it wasn't rest but recovery. Spending a few hours in my own place would settle the adrenaline high, but I couldn't rest long. My mother was still out there, and I needed to see Eustachys. Sleep was overrated anyway.

CHAPTER 8

A FEW HOURS' SLEEP for a college student is par for the course. The early afternoon sun spilled into my apartment bedroom. I yawned, stretched, and went straight to the bathroom. Clean teeth later, I picked up my phone and wandered to the kitchen.

My phone dinged with texts from Lilly, which I answered, and I caught another from the PI I'd hired.

Come in after 3 but b4 5.

I checked the time. Two seventeen.

Aliprand Eustachys, the guy I'd hired to find out any information about my mother, owned an office close enough to downtown that traffic was a factor. So, I tied a silk scarf around my neck, put on jeans, a white T-shirt, my sneakers and...

Crap. My car. It was still parked in a lone lot out in Timbuktu.

Diego had said he'd get it to me, but if I caught him at a good time, maybe he could give me a ride, and I'd make it to Aliprand's office in time.

I dialed Diego's number. As I waited for him to pick up, my eyes drifted to a familiar lump on my kitchen countertop. The keys to my car lay there like a coiled rattler.

Diego had been in my apartment without permission.

This violation disguised as convenience sent my heart rate thundering. Diego didn't knock on my door, leave the keys in the mailbox, or any other consideration. Nope. He'd come into my house sending a nonchalant message saying he could get to me at any time. That was a demon in essence. Their so-called "helpfulness" was an excuse to terrify. At least I hoped it was Diego because knowing Warren could stroll into my home would send me out of my mind. Treat me as a human...

Well, he wasn't going to get away with it. I was ready to spill my rage into Diego's ear.

He picked up, his voice sounding jovial, after the second ring. "Miles, did you find your car?"

"Listen, asshole, I do not appreciate you coming into my house without my permission no matter what good intention you have."

"Ummm... okay."

No, he was not going to act innocent this time. "You could have chosen another way to get my keys to me."

I heard a scuffing over the line as if he covered the microphone with his hand. Muffled voices carried out a conversation I couldn't make out except "You what?"

Diego came back on the line. "I understand, Miles. That won't happen again."

Click.

I pulled the phone back to my face. He'd hung up on me.

"Effer," I huffed. If I weren't in a rush, or I knew where to go, my anger might have driven me to storm his mansion and give him a piece of my mind. Instead, I grabbed my keys and checked the peephole to make sure a certain vampire wasn't stalking my front door.

Luck on my side, the hall was empty. Now to find my car. With the way my day was going, it'd be parked three blocks away, and I wouldn't find it until Eustachys was gone for the day. I should have asked Diego where he left my ride. Hell would freeze over before I called him again. At least today.

The street along my apartment was notorious for being busy. Parking was a joke. Nine times out of ten, I found a spot around the corner and walked half a mile to my door.

Remarkably, when I walked down the stairs, my car was front and center. The perfect spot, right in front of my stairs.

Of course. A demon can find premium parking. I'd never been able to get that close. Even moving in, I had to double-park. Demons probably did some of their voodoo magic to get good spaces. Unreal.

I walked up, only half believing it was my car, but I pushed the fob and the lights blinked and the doors unlocked. Yep. My car.

"Small miracles."

I folded myself onto the driver's side and checked under the passenger seat for my backpack. When my hand grabbed vinyl, a powerful wave of relief surged over my muscles. This faded bag was my life. Everything from a spare set of clothes to my wallet lived in this sack. The over-the-shoulder arm straps were thick and heavy and had seen a lot of wear, but they were intact and whole.

The one thing I wanted was small and metallic. I searched my jeans pockets first, then one of the compartments. It wasn't until I checked in a smaller pocket that I saw my laser pointer. I grabbed it, turned it on to see that it was still working, and breathed a sigh of relief.

After checking everything else was still in its place, I drove the "half hour" it took to get anywhere in this town and made it to Eustachys's office right at three.

Eustachys owned a five-story building that looked as ancient as he did. Heck, I was beginning to think he might have helped construct the thing back in the eighteen hundreds. It was one of the creepy, Gothic, a million windows, historic shrines that should have been a church. Thanks to zoning, the building could only be renovated no matter that it looked like it should be condemned.

I opened the creaking wood portcullis Eustachys called a door to the first-floor hall. The Nikes that Diego had given me squealed along the shiny black-and-white tile floor on my way to the stairs. The elevator was the original one that had been put in the building back when they came into style in the roaring twenties. I took the stairs because I could get to the fifth floor faster than waiting for the five minutes for the thing to get to ground level, then the five minutes it took to go up.

Plus, the verdict was still out about the lift attendant on whether he was human or not. The green pallor of his skin, and his flesh sagging like it was sloughing off, didn't make for a strong case on the "still alive" side.

This time around though, the stairs were tough. After two flights, I started getting out of breath. It might have been worth the extra time and smell of moth balls to ride the elevator.

Warren—that bastard of a Balrog—had sucked me dry. I wasn't out of shape. My body had taken a toll. His greed sparked an anger I'd only reserved for vampires. The burst of energy got me to the topflight of stairs. Dizzy and wheezing, I held on to the railing.

My burst of energy waned, but my rage lived inside me like a writhing snake.

Forgive and be forgiven.

Sometimes these phrases popped into my head. Mom had said it was my guardian angel watching over me. She'd also said that because we weren't solely human but not demons, we were assigned to the seraphim. The highest order of angels. Did I believe my mother? Hardly. If that were true, then why was my life so shitty.

When no clever rhyme bounced in my head, I mused to myself, "No answer for that one."

But in the very back of my mind, way, way beyond the tiny voice of intuition, I felt the warmth of a smile. It made me think of Michael, the priest from my dreams.

Ignoring the thoughts of insight, I stepped forward and brushed away my brown curls. I adjusted my scarf. Even if they weren't hiding bruised teeth marks, it had become a fashion statement. A habit. Ready for whatever he did nor did not find, I opened the classic PI office door.

"Mr. Eustachys?" I stepped into the reception room of the two-room office.

Even though he didn't have a secretary, his desk was in the back room.

"Miles? 'bout time." A tuft of white hair waved over the desk, and Aliprand Eustachys rose from underneath. What he was doing under his desk, I'd never ask. His wild dark eyes shifted back and forth. His wrinkles were more pronounced today. Aliprand was an thin elder man that reminded me of a shorter, devious Christopher Lloyd.

"What do you have for me?" I walked up like he didn't make me nervous, but he did. Especially when he smiled and flashed those crazy eyes. I imagined if he was human and didn't flinch or tell me vampires were a fable, then he'd probably seen enough crap to go bald and paranoid.

He smiled with perfect white block teeth. "Depends on what you might have for me."

Money. I did owe him. "Cash or card?"

"Either." He shrugged.

Since the money I had to pay with was in my bank account, I pulled out the plastic. My "woman card" had been challenged since I didn't carry a purse around, but a backpack carried more and didn't deter me while running from literal monsters.

"How much you want to put through?" He handed me the card reader.

"All of it." I put my card in the slot and waited.

Eustachys gave me a half-raised eyebrow, and the amount went through. "Guess the donor business pays well."

"When you give it all away it does," I mumbled.

His crazy eyes went narrow, and the look made his whole face go dangerous, but I got the impression it wasn't at me, but for me.

He didn't know the whole story about my gift. He did know I sold my blood to wannabe vampires. Lilly helped me find him because he was the only PI who didn't scoff at my request.

"So, what do you have?" I asked, before his curious mind could spin questions.

His feral grin and wild eyes returned. "Well, I can't call it conclusive, but it took me a while to find something."

"And?" Something was fine. Anything was better than nothing. Which was what I had. All my own leads were dead ends unless I bartered with Diego or Thomas. Going down that road was bad for my health.

He waved me around to the front of his desk and opened a laptop. A four-way split screen showed different locations around the city. Eustachys pounded on the keys, pausing one of the video screens of a busy sidewalk.

"Did you find her?" My excitement got away from me, and I scanned the crowd for my mother's face.

Eustachys tsked. "Kid, they aren't going to let your mother see the light of day." He sighed and rubbed the bald part of his head.

This time I flashed a glare at him. Did he know more than he let on?

He shrugged. "I had a run-in with one of the locals. I said the wrong thing and found myself sliding down the bar top. I haven't seen my contact since."

I winced. Anyone getting hurt on my account didn't sit well with me. "Local meaning supernatural?"

The right side of his mouth twitched. "Careful, kid, or you might end up like me."

"You mean suspicious and paranoid?" Too late.

He smirked. "Always at the wrong place at the wrong time."

"Oh, well, welcome to the club," I quipped.

"Watch this guy here." He pointed to a guy in a military jacket with lots of pockets and a black ball cap walking in a crowd of early morning pedestrians. He wasn't particularly outstanding. I recognized the street. It was in the district where tourists shopped for hemp socks, fanfare, and delicacies from around the world. The sea of suits and school kids indicated this was recorded during rush hour. Too early for vacationers.

Eustachys hit the Play button, and I watched Military Jacket guy. His head was down, covered by his hat. I couldn't make out anything about him.

"Oh... kay..." I scrunched my forehead at my PI. If he thought this was helpful, I was paying him too much.

"Watch." Eustachys kept looking at the screen, and I went back to watching but couldn't find him again.

"Where is he?"

My PI grinned like a manic Tasmanian devil. "Exactly. You took your eyes off him. That"—he raised a finger—"is exactly what you need to be looking for."

I huffed.

"Now watch him and keep watching him, if you can." He hit the space bar and backed up the video.

"Fine." I watched, but as the video played again, my mind wandered for half a second thinking about my mom. Where was she? Was she safe? Would they not let her see the light of day, like Eustachys said?

I went to focus on the screen, and the guy was gone. "Wait, I lost him again."

"Right." He gave me a sly grin. "Once more. Try to concentrate."

He backed up the video, and I let out a frustrated breath. I was starting to understand his point.

This time, I kept my mind blank and watched. A few moments in, my phone dinged, and I went for the new message. Like I was an errant customer, the wireless company reminded me of a payment due. I looked back to the screen… and couldn't find the Military Jacket dude.

"Ugh! Where is he?"

Eustachys eyed me, and I squirmed under his scrutiny. "It seems to work especially well on you," he said.

"I swear I'm not a flighty teenager that can't pay attention for more than three seconds." I couldn't even blame Warren for this one. Okay, I could but my low blood level was not the reason for my lack of attentiveness.

"Let's try this." Eustachys rewound the video and put his finger alongside the guy. "Watch my finger until I tell you, then I want you to look at him on the screen when I say now."

"I can watch him, I swear."

He shook his head. "Follow my finger, kid. It's not your fault."

Whatever that meant, but I acquiesced and Eustachys pressed Play.

I followed his finger as he slid it down the screen, following Military Jacket guy, though I admit it took discipline. This was the weirdest thing. I wanted to look anywhere else.

"Now!"

My eyes jumped to the screen, and it was a nanosecond when I saw a blurred face, and then he was gone. "What the heck!"

"That is what you're looking for, but it's hard to spot since you have the urge to look away, am I right?"

"Can you pause it right before he's gone?"

"That's the freaky part." Eustachys rewound the video three seconds and moved his finger along with the guy again. When he paused the video, the guy vanished.

"No, earlier."

Eustachys smiled, evil and mischievous. "He's still there, if you look especially close." He pointed, and I could make out a flat green elbow. The Military Jacket guy was behind another early morning suit.

"Wait, show me that again?"

Eustachys did. "If you look close, he fades, looks right, then goes left. It's a feint. I found it by chance and because I was looking for something else."

I looked him in the eye. "What am I seeing here?"

"That is a Florentine, and dollars to doughnuts, he's going into one of their sanctuaries."

"Okay, great. But I don't know what he looks like since everything is blocked or fuzzy."

"He went in this alleyway." Eustachys pointed to the identifiable corner of a side breeze large enough to fit nothing more than a Vespa. "I checked to see if he came out the other side, but he didn't. I think there's something there. That's where I'm going next. I wanted to update you."

"No." I shook my head. "Thank you, but I'll handle it." Because I already felt bad he'd gotten hurt on the job already.

"Kid, that could be dangerous. Could be a dead end. Let me handle it."

The way he refused to say "vampire" or call any of the supernatural their species name tipped me off. This job terrified him. He could cover it with his gruff manner and strong language, but I knew all about that kind of petrifying fear. The kind that fried your brain and kept your legs from working. Nightmares were kept at bay with denial. Sometimes. As much as Eustachys had seen, he was big in the denial that humans were not on top of the food chain. Disproving his strong held beliefs would shatter this brave man. This was my cross to bear. He was already getting too close.

"You're paid up." I patted him on the shoulder.

Eustachys gave me a dirty look and firmed his voice. "That's why I want to finish it, Miles."

He meant well. Even resorting to a stern browbeating and raising his voice. He cared, but she was my mother. We'd get out of this together, her and me.

"You got me something. I'll do the rest." I folded my arms. "Thank you, but I'll come back if it turns out to be a dead end. I don't need your help."

"Yeah. Right," he snorted. "Fine then, get outta my office."

His words didn't hurt. Acting the part of a bratty teenager helped adults save face. By telling him to stick his nose elsewhere meant he could in good conscious keep his honor intact.

Plus, I didn't need anyone's life in my hands. Trying to save me was a waste of time since I'd rejuvenate the next day. Or three. Fricking Warren.

I shut the door as I left and passed by the open elevator. The lift operator was standing there, looking out into space, half drooling with his hand on the control lever. Ghoul. Definitely. I opted for the stairs. Going down wasn't as hard as going up, but it still took effort.

CHAPTER 9

TAKING TIME OFF FROM donating was a luxury but complicated. Bloodletting in the wannabe vampire scene was a social thing. The more I showed my face, the more paying customers trusted me. Money was fleeting, about as fleeting as the red liquid in my veins within the fake vamp circles, but staking out a certain tourist corner for my mother this evening would result in nothing good. At best, men might think I was trading money for other parts of my body. At worst, I'd have to deal with Military Jacket guy at night.

I didn't go to the corner. By the time I left Eustachys, it was getting dark. Evening was not the time of day I wanted to confront a den of real vampires, or even one real familiar-to-me vampire that may or may not be waiting for me at my apartment complex.

Instead, I'd gone to Goth night at the coffee shop where all the regulars were meeting. It was only courteous that I let my clientele know I needed a break.

Cuppa Shot was one of those well-kept secrets. Most "Normans," our word for regular people, went to the glorified high-priced gift shop, sorry excuse of a retail store that happened to sell coffee-like syrup. The more refined, true coffee lovers went to the internet café where the lights were dimmed and people enjoyed steampunk sounds by Abney Park and Steam Power Giraffe from one of the dozen couches spread around the industrial warehouse. Bar-top tables and stools were also available to those who didn't want to swim in plush cushions.

Not that there was a war going on between small businesses and large corporations, but I liked to patronize the underdogs.

Cuppa Shot sported a ton of space and lots of people. Not all the tables were part of the vamp scene, so pretenses were downplayed. My popularity gave me choices and a plush chair to "hold court." These people prized me because I let them play out their fantasy, and play along I did. Also, getting the best chair in the house gave me warm fuzzies. The only person missing was Lilly.

Scott—my fellow student, this morning's ride, and my every other Tuesday client—walked up to my cushy throne. He puffed his chest out, looking like an Adam Lambert fan with brown eyes and dyed bright-red hair he had colored and spiked every which way, arranged to resemble a bird's nest. Behind him floated a cute dyed-burgundy redhead. Her hourglass figure would attract attention and jealousy. Especially with those electric blue eyes, though her heart-shaped face and eager smile would make her popular.

"Good evening, Liebling." Scott kneeled in front of me on one knee.

I wasn't into all the formal machinations of vampire society, fake or real, but I could give props for him paying respect. My little social group made sure I felt comfortable, and their efforts were appreciated.

"Hello, Scott. You've heard? I'm taking the next week off?"

He stayed in the kneeling position, eyes down, which meant he had official business. "I do know. I won't expect you till three weeks."

So formal. "Thank you. I appreciate it." The cute redhead beside him fidgeted with the laces of her bodice and wouldn't meet my eyes. She was nervous. Her short puffy black skirt covered the necessities to not be obscene. Her mismatched socks covered her legs to the thigh. Patton leather boots gave her a good inch lift.

"Who's your friend?" I asked.

Scott rose and took the redhead's hand. He pulled her in so I could get a good look. "This is Tika. I wanted to petition for her to be allowed into the fold."

"Ah, new girlfriend." I bobbed my head. "Nice to meet you, Tika."

She let out a breath, smiled, and curtsied. My acceptance calmed her nerves. She didn't have capped canines, which meant she wasn't looking for my services. Thank goodness. "It's nice to meet you, Miles."

"You're welcome here, but no drama. Everyone comes to de-stress, okay?"

Tika nodded. "Thank you, ma'am." She curtsied.

"Ugh! Call me Miles."

Tika cracked a smile so bright I could see why Scott was enamored with her.

"Thank you," she said, then added, "Liebling."

I rolled my eyes at my "official" title as Scott and Tika floated into the fray. I couldn't get any of them to stop calling me that. Pomp, circumstance, and manners were part of the scene, but they let me get away with plain speech and my ratty jeans, so I could let them call me by my given court title. Besides, it was good to be the favorite.

I wasn't taking customers tonight. Everyone knew it. It felt... normal. Which was strange. I didn't feel the jittery tiredness that went with anemia.

Then, as my luck would have it, Thomas walked in.

"Crap," I uttered. My stomach fell to the bottom of my feet.

All eyes turned to him. No, that wasn't accurate. Everyone from my group of fake vampires turned to Thomas and stared at him as if he were a king. The Normans paid no attention to him.

Thomas hadn't seen me as he walked up to the register, and I contemplated sneaking out. Here, though, around people meant I was relatively safe.

Thomas sniffed the air like a blood hound as he waited for his order, and our eyes met. He had on his yellow contacts again, but he let his real fangs hang down over his lower lip. His stare pinned me to my seat, and he spoke sideways to the barista all while keeping my gaze.

Fear crashed into the intersection of rational thought and screamed, Get the heck out of here. However, I remained seated in my plush armchair. If Military Jacket guy was a dead end, there was always Thomas. Screw Diego. I was not going to deal with him or Warren again. Ever.

After a hot minute, he grabbed two porcelain cups and saucers and headed my way.

Oh crap, crap, crap. No, don't come over here.

As he made his way, a path cleared for him. The Normans turned the other way, giving him a wide berth. One person stopped, as if in confusion and trying to regain his focus. Another woman that nearly crossed Thomas's beeline path jerked to a halt and started typing on her phone, letting the vampire pass by.

I hadn't noticed at the rave, but the other Goth wannabes tipped their head in deference to him, like they knew he was the real thing. Thomas was not a fairy tale.

People threw covert glances between Thomas and me. The effect raised the tiny hairs on my neck.

"Miles," Thomas drawled like a cowboy CEO. He dropped to one knee in front of my chair and held a coffee within arm's reach like a white knight offering me his sword.

All the Goths' attention zoomed in on me. Jealous stares and awestruck gazes alike sent chills down my spine.

He waited while I took it all in.

"Espresso macchiato," he said. "I hear it's your favorite."

I focused on the vampire before me. He was in full regalia. His immaculate suit fit every nook and cranny of his muscled body. That fanged smile of his flashed in dangerous mischief. Not a hair out of place. He could come straight out of a movie screen and charm the pants off any unsuspecting mortal.

"Thank you, but I'll get my own," I said.

Someone close enough to hear me chuffed.

His smile faltered and turned brittle. "Miles, I come in peace."

I rolled my eyes at his line and lowered my voice. "Then let the real Thomas speak."

Without moving his lips, he said, "Do you remember what I said about expectations?"

That's right. In the hall, he said this side of his persona wasn't genuine and alluded to social pressures. People edged closer, probably thinking they disguised themselves well when it was obvious they wanted to hear our conversation. Nobody outright stared, but the glimpses and whispers gave them away. We were entertainment.

Even if he had on his yellow contacts, the tiredness around his eyes went deep. I took the offered coffee for his sake. Partially because I was a sucker. The foolhardy kind, not the siphoning kind.

"There, your reputation is intact." I took a sip of coffee.

His smile turned genuine giving him sex appeal. "Some things are worth the tarnish."

In that moment, he could have been Thomas, boyfriend material.

Careful, Miles, I cautioned myself. Vampires do a good job of imitating life. They got behind the trenches and ripped apart whatever trust they'd gained at the opportune moment.

I rolled my eyes at him and leaned in conspiratorially. "What would they ever think if they knew you had crystal-blue eyes?"

"If that's what it takes to get a taste of you, then I'd toss the contacts in the trash right now," he purred.

I responded with a raised eyebrow.

"Okay, yeah, that sounded better in my head." He chuckled.

It made me laugh. "Be honest, you've wanted to ditch them for some time."

He huffed. "Yeah, yeah, the eighties called and want their vampire back."

I raised my hands. "Hey, you said it, and wow, you are old."

"Why thank you." He gave a flourish over his chest. "But"—he turned serious—"are you all right?"

A sigh escaped my lips as I nodded. Despite the small talk, the tension in my shoulders wouldn't let me relax. "I'll be fine."

I was well compensated for dying, but it's not something I liked to practice every day, or in any lifetime.

Thomas roamed his gaze over my face with part awe, part longing. "I can't help but ask, while in the hall of our apartments, you mentioned a proposition. Was that fear-based or something more substantial?"

Oh crap. The climb of tension dropped to my stomach. I should have expected it. I'd asked, and he seemed reasonable to possibly trade information for blood. How screwed up was this scenario?

He was still kneeling before me. We were starting to get a lot of stares even from the Normans.

"Ummm... I'd like to maybe talk where people aren't gawking."

"Right. Did you want to go back home?"

Nope. "Here is fine."

I eyed an empty table in the corner. It terrified me being alone with a vampire in a dark corner, but Thomas was my option for more information. Time taught me that only one avenue wasn't enough. Not when it came to finding my mother.

He looked back to where I pinned my gaze. "That's fine."

Thomas rose taking my coffee cup out of my hands and waited for me to get up. I stood and made a beeline for the one private table away from most everyone. Before we got there, a group of four jock-types sat in the chairs of our unclaimed spot. I stopped dead immediately relieved but looking for another place to go. Thomas didn't stop. He kept going to our chosen table.

"We can find another table," I said.

But Thomas didn't acknowledge me.

The four guys looked college age and probably went to my university. The way they were casting their eyes made it clear they were looking at Goth girls. Guys like them sometimes had a fetish for the unusual. They paid no mind to the vampire walking straight for them.

I hurried over to Thomas's side, my heart pounding because I wasn't sure what his reaction would be. Vampires were similar to humans, but they had strange behaviors. Their logic was a little "off."

Thomas went right up to the four and started growling. It wasn't the sound a dog made but the low rumble of a tiger. The four Normans stared at Thomas, then glanced at each other.

"Leave," Thomas said.

He was crazy. There were four of them. If they decided they weren't going to comply, what then? Vampires were strong, but did he have the chops to beat them all down?

Turned out, I didn't have to worry. The four frat boys scrambled to get away from the table and all the way out of the building as if their life depended on it.

Interesting. "I see you're as charming to humans as you are your own kind."

Yellow eyes slid over me, but he said nothing. He nodded to the stool in the corner, and I balked. Corners were for cats and rats.

"I'll take this seat." I pulled out the chair closest to the exit.

Thomas narrowed his eyes, and his shoulders went stiff. He acted as if I'd offended him.

"I'm claustrophobic," I said. "If I sit there, I'll well up with the past, a past that isn't so good. If you want me to hear anything you say, then give me fast access to the exit."

His features softened and acquiesced and let me have my seat.

"You are so unusual, Miles." Thomas set both coffee cups on the table and sat in the corner. "It makes me curious."

He cast his gaze at me, and I sipped my coffee so that I wouldn't look into his eyes. A vampire's stare was dangerous, but Thomas's yellow contacts were disturbing.

After a moment of collecting my thoughts, I looked up into his eyes. Big mistake. My stomach quivered. I focused on his chin instead. No use in thinking too much. Just jump right in.

"So, I want to make a trade."

He waited, not filling in the blanks. It occurred to me that straight up asking for Eli Florentine might be a red flag. Like asking around might tip him off and then have the Florentine den move once again because I was asking too many questions. This time, I was going to be smart.

"I want to trade for information."

Thomas didn't balk or even bring up the fact that I'd changed the trade terms from this morning.

"I agree," he said.

"Whoa, whoa, whoa..." I held up my hands, and this time I did look into his fierce gaze. He didn't give anything away, but his eager compliance said he was anything but apathetic. "You don't want to know what information or what I'm trading?"

"That's not how this works, Miles," he drawled out my name like his tongue was having sex with the syllables.

My instincts went haywire. I wanted to throw the chair at him and run home. The coffee in my stomach turned to sludge. Every effort of my being went into not throwing up.

"Miles?" Thomas gritted his teeth. "Please..." he swore, his voice soft as he said, "This is why I wanted you in the corner. I knew this would happen."

He was reacting to me. Every time I started freaking out, he went off the deep end. This was a me thing. I had to get control of myself. Yes, I had an enclave suckle at my every main vein from the time I was five years old until I escaped. Yes, I had scars over my heart, my mind, and my body to prove it, but it was time to get over that crap. I was stronger than this.

Calm. Breathe. Steady my heartbeat. That's what Thomas said this morning and that's what I needed to do now. I closed my eyes and took slow and steady breaths. Trusting that Thomas wouldn't attack me in front of a crowd.

When I opened my eyes, I was still trembling, but I wasn't ready to bolt. Thomas gripped the table, his fingers leaving indents in the wood, which made me think that maybe he was strong enough to handle a group of jocks.

"Better?" I asked.

"Yes," he hissed through his teeth. "But I don't like being played with." He stood and adjusted his tie. "When you have an offer you can back up, call me."

He went to go around me, but I reached out and pinched his sleeve. "Wait!"

Thomas stopped, but those yellow eyes and his reproaching gaze drew me back.

"Please..." I let regret flow into my voice. "I know I seem educated, but the reality is that I only know what I remember." I had to make this good to make him stay. "My first memory ever was waking in the dark. I think I was in a crib, but it might well have been a cage. I couldn't move. There were people, too many to count, with fangs dripping red liquid. Then I remember being lifted, then pain. If that's what you are, if you find it normal to eat babies, then you're right, I have nothing to bargain and nothing more to say to you ever again."

The admittance shocked me. That was not what I was going to say. I thought an apology would suffice, but I had to know if vampires were the soulless monsters I remembered them as. I shuddered at the memory.

Thomas stood there staring. "How old were you?"

I shrugged. "Maybe five."

Not like my birthday was celebrated even though Mother tried to give me a semblance of human life. The heavy weight of memories settled on my shoulders.

He sat and folded his hands in front of him.

I took another sip of my coffee, then said, "I hope you understand that sometimes I panic."

Thomas stared at me like the anomaly I was, not that he knew quite the extent.

"I was enclave property until I was almost twelve," I said. Crap. I was running at the mouth and didn't know when to quit. "And that's all I'm going to say about it."

Thomas kept staring, and it was starting to freak me out.

"Ummm... okay..." I pulled out my wallet and set down a five-dollar bill. "Here's for the coffee."

He looked down and that broke his reverie. "When you want to broker a deal with a vampire, state what you want, then let your opponent state what they want. That's how it works."

"Oh." I snuggled back into my seat. He was talking, and this was the helpful kind of interaction.

"You want information," he said. "I want your company. I'll trade with you in person, no phone calls and on my terms. That means I can refuse a question, and where we meet will be my choice."

If he thought I was a push over in dealmaking, he was sorely mistaken. "I want to know in advance where we'll meet and right of refusal."

His eyes went wide then half lidded, hopefully not catching onto my lack of naivety. "I agree to those terms. Anything else?"

"I need to feel safe. We must meet in public."

Thomas deflated, and his eyes crinkled in concern. "Of course." Then he grimaced. "So that you know, I offered you the corner seat for a strategic reason, but for you, I can ignore the slight."

I huffed. "That is some stupid vampire etiquette. If you want someone to feel comfortable, you allow them to choose their seat."

"Ahhh..." He lifted his index finger and circled it with austere authority. "But you are human. Placing you in the corner proves I trust you to watch my back. It also allows me to protect you, or at the very least act as a shield, while making a route for your escape. I can react faster, turn around faster, and in that position, I can shield you better."

Okay, that did make sense in a very archaic way. "What I believe you're also saying is that it's not normal to eat a five-year-old."

His face soured. "Last freebie, then you agree or deny this arrangement and only because I don't want you to have the wrong impression, which you clearly do. No, it is not okay to eat five-year-olds. It's disgusting. But, let's just say..." He gritted his teeth. "There are some that like veal. I personally find it revolting."

Good to know he wasn't part of the Florentine vampires. Those mother effers were vicious. "Then I agree to your terms until I don't."

Thomas narrowed his eyes. "That's insulting. Rephrase that or I revoke my agreement."

"You can do that?"

"The correct phrase is 'I agree to the terms as they are; we can revisit them at any time.'"

"How do any of you trust one another?"

"Fair question. But as I said, no more freebies."

I snorted. "Fine. I agree to the terms as they are; we can revisit them at any time."

"Very good." He dipped his head my way. "I agree to the terms as they are; we can revisit them at any time."

I felt a tingle in my body that gave power to my words. "Ack! Are these pacts karma infused or something?"

Thomas tilted his head. "Karma. You could say there is a certain truth to that, yes." He snapped a breath inward. "Did you actually feel the tie taking hold?"

"Like a tingling."

His eyes went wide. The yellow contacts went all the way around his sclera. "Heh. You, my dear, have a bit of demon in your family tree."

I was too anxious to take that bait. "Alright. First question. Explain the whole sunlight thing. I mean, you were up during the bright morning, and it wasn't early." Plus, he'd gone tumbling down the stairs, and I knew there was daylight at the bottom.

"Grossly blown out of proportion by movies." Thomas sat back down and took a sip of his coffee.

"You can walk in daylight?"

"There is a difference between not wanting to go in the sun and can't go out in the day," he chuckled. "Can you imagine all the night workers. No, we try to blend in, not stick out. Refusing to go out in daylight would be one heck of a red flag."

"And you can at least drink normal things." I looked at his coffee.

He set down his cup. "Liquid is different from solids. No, I can't have a blueberry muffin. That's cause to throw up, but liquid can be digested. It doesn't give us what we need from blood, but people get uncomfortable when you don't eat or drink anything. Thus..." He lifted his drink.

"Garlic?"

"Seriously, garlic? Onions? Do you want to kiss someone that reeks?"

"Silver?"

"Ah, that one is complicated. It must be inherited silver, not any silver would be enough. It has to have meaning."

"Stake to the heart?"

Thomas rolled his eyes. "If I drove a stake through your heart or cut off your head, would you live?"

Yeah, I didn't want to test any of those theories on myself. "Alright, smarty pants, let's get to more technical questions. There are some fictional vampires that don't kill. How much blood do you actually need?"

Thomas sobered. He looked like a professor about to give a lecture. His unblinking stare was enough to make me tell him to forget it and move on. He finally answered, "You must think all of us are monsters, and from what you've been through, I don't blame you. But how can you sit there, talk to me, show emotion, intelligence, and think that I can snuff out sentient life like that? If our roles were reversed, could you slit my throat and cook me over a stove? Does life mean that little to you?"

Oh. That's a perspective.

His lips pinched giving him a perturbed air. "I'll ask you, how many plants and animals have you destroyed to sate your need?"

He stared at me, but I wasn't going to let him become high-and-mighty about it.

"What I'm hearing is that when you kill, it's even worse because you don't actually need to, you like to."

Thomas crossed his arms and shifted his eyes away.

Ha! I was not going to cow over this moral dilemma.

"Part of being human means living in this conundrum," I said. "You might be proud that you may or may not have a kill count to survive, but you don't live it, so don't get haughty."

He turned a wary eye to me. Point to Thomas for not tossing his arrogance in my face.

Then I heard a pop to my left, and a familiar, terrifying voice growled, "You, again!"

Before I could react, Thomas was pinned up against the wall.

CHAPTER 10

"WHAT HAVE YOU DONE!" Warren Coroner held Thomas against the wall by his neck.

Thomas hissed, bared his teeth, and kicked at the very person I never wanted to see again. Warren confined the other vampire with his large hands, squeezing the life out of him, all while looking like a business gangster with his silk suit, flashy tie, and crisp white shirt.

I jumped up, tipping my stool that went crashing to the ground. "What are you doing?"

Warren ignored me and growled at Thomas, "I said to leave her."

"Get off him!" Even as I said the words, and meant them, a gratifying sliver fizzled in my chest. The notion that someone so powerful, as misguided as he was, would protect me sent warmth to my heart.

Shocked, awed faces from the vamp community stared back at me. Oddly, the Normans were talking and walking around like none of this was happening. The dichotomy of these two worlds gave me pause.

Thomas clawed at the fingers pressed against his neck and squirmed to break free while flashing two-inch fangs. He was pissed.

Everyone else was too shocked to move, but I wasn't going to sit here and let Warren bully my new acquaintance.

"Stop, you butt munch!" I lunged forward and struck Warren's backside with an ineffective slap.

At my words, Warren turned his neck, his face incredulous. "Butt munch?"

Any other time I'd laugh, but the seriousness pushed all amusement out of the situation.

"Let him go!"

"I'm not hurting him. His air is cut so he can't talk and weave more agreements from you."

How did he know. How much had he seen? "They are my agreements to make."

"He's taking advantage of your naivety." He shook Thomas and thumped his back against the plaster.

"Thomas is telling me information I need to know."

"You shouldn't need to know anything from him!" Warren's height and reach prevented the smaller vampire from clawing at his face, though it didn't stop Thomas from trying. He waved his arms, trying to make any contact, but Warren was built like a monster. Tall, lanky yet he was broad enough to fill a doorway. His strength endless. Unfortunately, it was also sexy.

"You don't get to tell me what to do. Let him go, or I'll call the police." I heaved the words.

"Go ahead. It won't save him," Warren huffed.

Yeah, by the time they got here, anything could happen. "Don't."

Warren turned to Thomas. "I meant everything I said. You are becoming a nuisance."

Thomas struggled and gagged. He was trying to speak but was unable to. I had to do something. Just because Thomas was blood dependent didn't mean he deserved to die.

"You said you weren't responsible for me. If you meant it, then why are you even here?"

Warren dropped his load and sneered at me. "I didn't know it was going to be like this."

What the hell is he talking about? "Not my problem."

He turned back to Thomas and loomed over him. "What did you have her agree to?"

"I'm... answering... questions," Thomas choked out, adjusting his tie.

"In exchange for what?" Warren grabbed at the other vampire's suit and hauled him to eye level.

"Her time." Thomas grabbed Warren's wrists and held on.

Thomas's answer was, apparently, the wrong one.

Warren's body became a miasma of darkness. Swirling black ash, formed in the shape of Warren's body.

"No!" Thomas screeched. "No! I haven't touched her!"

"Warren?" I froze. The night in the limo came back. The monster of ash and fire. Was he going to eat Thomas? "What are you doing?"

Warren pulled Thomas into himself—into the churning ash part of his body, reminding me of a dark hole.

Thomas struggled, screeching, but there was nothing for him to hold on to, nothing to help him resist being pulled into the darkness.

"Warren!" It was all I could say. "He's telling the truth."

My words were no use. Warren grabbed the back of Thomas's head, pushed him into his ash-like body, and then the vampire was gone.

"No!" I lunged forward. "What did you do?"

Warren grabbed my arm and hauled me back, saving me from crashing into his solid body.

"He'll be fine." Warren pulled me along, my coffee left behind.

"Where did he go?" My steps reluctant, anyone with a brain would know I wasn't leaving of my own volition. Pure shock made me compliant.

Several fake vampires hissed and exposed their teeth, Scott among them.

"No!" I held my hand up. I didn't want any of them hurt. "It's okay. I'll be okay."

Warren side-eyed me and sneered. "You think I'm the evil doer?"

"Let her go!" Scott stepped forward, showing his dentist drilled enamel fangs.

Oh, no. Warren would kill him.

"Scott, it's okay. I can handle this."

My every-other-Tuesday appointment wasn't deterred. "She's ours, unless she claims you into the fold, unhand her."

Warren let go and turned to me. "Fine. I want no part of your enclave."

He turned and stormed out of the coffee shop. Long strands of his hair flared out as he went. If he wasn't such a jerk, he'd be as beautiful as a reverse Fabio.

Everyone in my group crowded around me, involving me as the center of their group hug. Some were trembling. Others held me tight for a moment and passed me to another. They were silent with the exceptions of the occasional whispered "Liebling." Most said nothing, giving me words through the concern in their eyes. Dozens of hands touched my hair and shoulders as if I were a good luck charm.

This group was a little strange sometimes. Sweet and unique, that's how I thought of them.

Scott pulled up beside me, his smirk insufferable. "I thought you said you didn't sleep with suckers."

"What?" Everyone was being ridiculous. Like their hero being pushed into a void was normal. "I don't sleep with clients." I primly corrected his language.

My patron's eyebrows lifted so high it wrinkled his forehead. "The echelon was clearly jealous. There might not be something between you two, but he doesn't know that."

Ugh! "Why are you defending him? He threw your idol into some portal." Thomas could be lost in a freezer locker or inside of Warren for all I knew. Dang it. My consciousness wasn't going to lay off. If Thomas was in danger, then I couldn't stand by and do nothing.

Scott threw up his hands. "I'm not defending him. Only the desperate and crazy get involved with the Coroner."

"Well, I'm not alone in my madness. You stepped in it as well."

Scott gave a sideways glance to Tika. She was looking at Scott like he was the moon that hung the stars. Oh, I see.

"I was only protecting my donor," he said.

More like trying to impress the girlfriend. "You know Warren?"

Scott shook his head. "I know of the Coroner."

How unexpected. "You still stuck your neck out for me. Thank you."

He blushed and rubbed a hand along the back of his neck. "The Coroner isn't prone to hurt humans." Scott passed a critical eye over me.

If I didn't know better, I'd think he was calling me out as a demon. Maybe I was. The jury was still out. That notion created a band of anxiety around my chest and squeezed.

"I need to make sure Thomas is okay."

"You sure you want to get in the middle of that?" He waved a hand to the door.

I feared I was already involved. "I have to go, Scott. See you in three weeks?"

He nodded as I left. The rest of the clique watched me go without protest. Thank goodness.

Good thing I turned in the right direction. I saw Warren in the distance. His long legs had carried him down two blocks. He was walking toward the coffee shop, head down, hands in his coat and obviously concentrating inward. He didn't see me. The sidewalk was empty, and I started jogging to catch up.

"Hey!" I yelled out.

Warren stopped and waited. His eyes sparked with hopeful vulnerability. When I got close enough, he scanned the area. Right. He'd asked me not to mention him to anyone. Well, too bad. He'd come into the coffee shop disturbing my conversation with Thomas. That was on him. I was fully prepared to never see Warren Coroner again, except in my nightmares, but I was drawn to him.

Warren's left eye twitched. "Were you testing me?"

"What?" What is he talking about? Is Scott right, and Warren thought we were an item? "Because I was with Thomas?"

He slashed his hand through the air. "I don't give a damn about Thomas."

Time to be articulate. "Then why are you coming into public places and tossing him into the big black yonder?" I waved my hand at Warren.

"Because you are driving me out of my mind!" He threw his hands up. "No. You know what," he growled. "You owe me an explanation."

"Me?" I pulled back. "Explain what?"

He ground his teeth. "How about because I'm now bound. You haven't even told me the terms! You"—he pointed at me—"you are the reason I don't keep blood bonds."

I had no idea what he was talking about, but I spat back, "And that would be a reason to drain me to death?"

"That was a mistake." He looked away, slumping his shoulders.

"You have nobody to blame but yourself."

He huffed and took a step back. "Fair. But I need to know what deal you made."

"Where is Thomas?"

"Thomas is fine. I dropped him off at his own apartment."

Warren's white limo pulled up alongside.

Great. Now Diego was here too.

"What business is it of yours what agreement I made with him?" How did he know I made an agreement at all? Was he spying on me?

He pulled back, eyes wide, like he didn't believe a word I said. He bared sharp and pointed teeth and narrowed suspicious eyes. "Because I'm now bound by it too."

"That makes no sense." I stared at him. "It's my agreement with him, not yours."

Warren stepped forward. "Tell me, or I will ask him."

His whisky-and-honey voice sent a shiver of pleasure down my spine. But his connotation left no doubt he'd flay the skin from Thomas's bones to get an answer.

A heartbeat went by while calculating our terms and if I was breaking my end of the bargain by telling someone. "We meet, and he answers my questions."

"That's all?" His suspicion clear in his red-gold eyes.

"Yes."

Warren pulled back, his lips pursing. "Could have asked me."

His shoulders dropped as we stared at each other.

My heart thrummed a beat in my chest playing to a soundless earworm. The annoying thing was that I didn't know the lyrics to this song.

"I would see you safe back to your apartment." His words lingered in the air.

Neither of us moved. It was night. I was tired. I wanted to get up early in the morning. Time usually spent recovering from blood loss was now freed up because of Warren. For that I was grateful.

"If I argue?" I folded my arms.

"Then I will follow out of your sight." He straightened and adjusted his tie.

Of course he would. "Stalker much?"

He let out an exasperated breath and within it whispered, "Don't compare me to my mother."

The thought of what Warren's mother might be like gave me goose bumps.

He turned to the limo and walked to the driver's side. The window rolled down, but at this angle, I couldn't confirm it was Diego who steered the massive boat of a car. He said a few words then returned to my side.

"Where are you parked?" He waved a hand for me to start moving.

"This way." I turned back to Cuppa Shot's parking lot and made my way to my blue Honda. Warren signaled his driver, and the white limo crept beside us to the aggravation of traffic. No horns blew, but plenty of cars passed the stretched BMW with a roaring engine.

I pulled out my keys with a shaky hand when we approached my car.

His lips a thin line, he set his hand upon mine. "Are you comfortable riding with me?"

I turned back to him, feeling the sincerity of his words. He'd thought of the attack in his limo and anticipated my concern. He did have courtesy after all.

"Not really."

Warren's eyes darted away. His head lowered, and the weight of shame settled along his shoulders.

"Then we will follow." Warren backed away, taking the warmth of his hand with him.

"No." I almost grabbed for him but stopped short, surprised on how clear my command came out. "I want you to confirm what Thomas said."

For all his faults, everything he'd done, Warren spoke honestly. That was worth more than he knew. His ability to suss out falsehoods, lies, and certainties was uncanny. I don't know how he did it, but the first time we met in his underground church, he'd been able to tell when I was lying. I'd convinced Diego of my tale, but not Warren.

"You are very brave, Liebling." Warren took my keys from my hand and opened the driver's door for me and set the keys in the ignition.

I slipped inside my car and opened the passenger lock for him as he crossed to the other side. He folded himself in the passenger seat adjusting to accommodate his tall frame, buckled his seatbelt like he'd been told how to strap in, but never actually done it before, and had to tilt the seat so far back it looked like he was preparing for a nap.

"Comfortable?" A smile slid past my defenses.

The boyish smirk lifted years off his face. "Not really."

"Too bad," I joked.

A deep rumbling laugh thrummed from his chest. It eased my nerves knowing that he could find humility.

When Cuppa Shot was out of sight, he asked, "What answers do you seek?"

A lump went down along with a gulp of anxiety. "I was asking about vampire myths."

He didn't prompt me and waited.

"He told me he wanted me in the corner seat so I could watch his back, and he could protect me."

"But you were facing the wall."

"I'm a little claustrophobic. He let me take the other seat."

"Hmmm..."

Not the answer I was looking for. "Is it true?"

He sighed. "It's true that you believe that's what he said to you. It's true you believed him. It's true you are claustrophobic, and it's true he allowed you the other seat. But I cannot tell if his explanation was true. I wasn't there."

"You need to hear the words spoken to tell." Not a question, my observation.

"To tell if what he says is true? Yes."

Interesting. "But is what he said true?"

"What did he say, verbatim?"

After I reiterated Thomas's explanations, Warren confirmed he was telling the truth about everything else too, which was frightening.

"What about all the vampire myths? Isn't there some truth to any of them?"

"Of course." Warren stretched out on my passenger seat, getting comfortable. "But your perception of vampires is clouded by what's portrayed in the movies."

"Then enlighten me." The more we conversed, the more Warren relaxed. Seeing him nearly flat in the seat beside me made him less threatening. He could grab me in a flash, I was sure of that, but sprawled out like a fluffy house cat, showing his belly couldn't be more submissive and comforting.

"First, the word vampire is about the same as saying 'thing that drinks blood'." There are numerous beings sustained on blood, like lawyers, bankers, slave traders, and career politicians."

I smiled, searching his face checking that it was indeed a joke. When he flashed blocky white teeth, I laughed.

"You have a sense of humor," I said. His presence became less of a nightmare and more a high-school sophomore's dream. "But I was talking about the kind like Thomas."

"Ah." He put his hands behind his head. "You are talking about Dracules."

"Like Count Dracula?"

Warren huffed. "Vlad Tepes is whom you refer. He was a madman but also deserves respect. He saved the human race by brutalizing half his enclave. They wanted to enslave humans. Tepes felt extreme measures needed to be taken, and it worked."

"You're rewriting history now?"

"Believe my words or stop asking questions." His tone grew cold.

Shoot. I'd insulted him. Warren didn't need to tell me anything. If other blood drinkers existed, I wanted to know their differences.

"I'm sorry. I didn't mean to offend you. But..." How ancient is he? I looked over at his face. Who knew what an old demon looked like. It's not like they got wrinkles with age.

"Tell me," Warren sighed. "What is it you are looking for?"

Words caught in my throat. My heart sank and then sped up. Sweat coated my palms. I swallowed and noticed goose bumps raising the hairs on my arms. Here was my chance to get answers. Surely Warren knew of the Florentine vampires. Sorry, Dracules.

The demon beside me turned in his seat the best he could with the car's lap belt over his hips.

"You are not required to answer," he whispered, "if it causes you this much distress. In fact, please don't. I probably wouldn't like the answer anyway." He lay flat and crooked his head to the window.

When I drove up to my apartment, I stared at the huge empty parking space in front of the stairwell to the alcove of my home. I blinked several times and squinted to make sure the opening was not a mirage. I saw enough room for my car and the limo following behind. I swerved into the closest spot, forcing Diego to park that massive white BMW in front of my vehicle.

I watched in fascination as the limo backed in with more expediency than safety. Diego maneuvered from the driving lane next to the curb in one smooth transition. Of course he did. Who knew demons could be expert drivers.

Warren opened his door and unfolded himself from my car. He waited for me with arms crossed standing in front of my apartment complex and avoided looking at me.

"Shall we?" He motioned to the stairs of my apartment. "It's late."

I locked my car and followed him up, allowing him to go first. When he got to the top, he scowled at Thomas's door.

Wanting to make sure Thomas was okay, I tried stepping up to knock when Warren immediately pushed me back.

I squawked, "Hey! I want to see if he's okay!"

"He's fine."

"How do you know?"

"Because he's sniveling behind his door."

Oh dear. If Thomas was behind the door, this would get ugly fast. "That's not—"

Thomas's door flew open so fast it was a wonder it didn't fly off the hinges. "Here I am, Adam's son."

Wait. What did he call Warren? Adam's son. As in the first man, Adam? I'll need to find out about that.

Warren growled a mirthless laugh. "Don't pretend to be my match. You're only alive out of mercy."

Thomas was furious. His teeth were two-pronged, short pointers in front, long pointies right behind them. His eyes sparkled in maleficent revulsion. This might end with one of them dead.

Thomas wouldn't let this challenge go, even if he were up against the monster of all vampires. Or whatever Warren was. Two predators were about to pounce on each other, and I could do nothing to stop them.

Like a whisper, Scott popped into my mind. The echelon was clearly jealous.

"Warren, stop." My words were spoken like a command. To a blood drinker, they were no more than a plea.

By some miracle, Warren ratcheted down his hostility, turned an eye to me, and lifted a brow.

Thomas took his withdrawal poorly. "Don't you dare treat me like a secondary concern, cretin."

Dang it, Thomas! Shut your mouth. For the love of peace, I wished a vampire—sorry, Dracule—would take the win for once.

No warning, not even a flash—one moment Warren was by my side, the next nanosecond, Thomas was being pushed face-first against his own hallway entry.

"You owe your miserable existence to her."

This time Warren bared teeth. Something I didn't notice before, mostly because I was scared out of my wits, but Warren's teeth weren't the same double canines like a usual Dracule. His were a full set of mako shark teeth.

"Go... ahead..." Thomas struggled for breath. "Eat me... freak."

"Since you asked..." Warren growled.

"No." I was proud my voice didn't waver. "He's done nothing wrong."

"Except piss me off," Warren snarled.

"If your anger is for my sake, don't bother." I had to be calm. No emotion would help right now. I took the panic, the fear, and shoved them down like oversized socks.

Warren rumbled like a tiger about to strike but amazingly eased off Thomas. Holy mackerel. Warren listened to me. This massive individual let me dictate the outcome of the interaction. He let me decide. Relief came in an instant, and I let out a sigh.

Warren snorted, "I was not that out of control."

My neighbor took his time sliding down the wall to pool in a shaking mess in his own hallway.

I'd never seen a vampire so terrified. They usually didn't show anything but a masculine version of strength. While stoic silence was an admirable trait, I wasn't used to seeing the feminine power of vulnerability. Not in a creature like Thomas.

"I thought you were going to lick his face and go full Hannibal." I resisted helping Thomas get up. His reputation was already damaged.

All of Warren's seven-foot frame shuddered in revulsion.

"I don't like to." He glared at Thomas. "But I will drain a demon when needs must."

Blooming respect unfurled in my chest replacing the fear as I began to understand Warren more. He'd given me something I'd never felt I had. Control. Better yet, his trust in me was a heady feeling. It presented a conundrum. Mr. Coroner was complicated. I wanted to know him, even if he'd proven himself a little too dangerous for comfort.

Hunger was a valid motivator. Killing me wasn't going to ever be justifiable, but if what Diego said was true and Warren had starved himself, then admonishing him for drinking my blood was like Thomas scolding me for eating meat.

Warren smiled at me like he'd heard the entire conversation I'd had with myself. His red-gold eyes softened. Warmth and affection replaced the sorrow and loneliness I'd seen when we first met, and it was—beautiful. Like butterfly wings fluttering against my heart. The fondness was there for an instant, then it was as if he caught himself and turned an annoyed glance away and wouldn't look at my face.

"There's no other explanation." Thomas picked himself up, trying to regain his dignity. "You... He drank from you." Thomas leaned close to his door ready to bolt it closed. "I don't understand how you're not—"

Warren stepped up letting loose a rumble, cutting Thomas's sentence off. "Don't you dare petition her."

Thomas smiled with his annoying signature smirk. "That would be up to Miles."

"I will not have you in her enclave."

Okay, wut? Petition? For blood? I don't have an enclave. That is a Dracule thing.

They both stared at me like I had a clue. Assuredly, I didn't have a ball of string or much less, a shred of yarn, to guide me through this maze.

"Of course." Warren pinched the bridge of his nose.

Thomas, on the other hand, started with a half-hearted chortle that turned into a vibrant laugh. When he could regain himself, he said, "She doesn't know, does she? That's why all the amateur questions."

"You know what, I'm starting to think Warren is right. I don't need you."

Warren stared at me, surprise on his face.

"Have fun with that," Thomas snarled, shutting his front door, leaving Warren alone with me in the apartment complex foyer.

After a moment's silence and Warren eyeing me with suspicion, I flung my hand toward my neighbor's apartment. "What don't I know?"

"A great many things," Warren rumbled.

His sexy voice pulled on my insides. If he wasn't terrifying, a girl might want to explore what kinds of noises he could make. Something gave me away because Warren lifted an eyebrow, and his interest intensified.

"Care to fill me in?" I folded my arms.

Warren studied my mouth and smiled widely. "Let's get you safely into your room."

My stomach dropped to my knees, and yet I nearly fell with the strength of my lust. He wasn't planning on coming in, was he? I wasn't sure if I'd screw him or fear for my life if he walked into my apartment. "I'll be fine."

He turned to face me but didn't otherwise move. "Your caution is... absurd," he said.

"Oh? You think it's absurd that I'm weary of your teeth on my neck again? It's absurd that I remember you threatened to kill me when I—"

He was towering over me in a flash with his finger pressed to my lips, his mouth at my ear. The last of my breath squeaked out of my lungs.

Whispering so low I could scarcely hear him say, "Are you sure it's my teeth you're worried about?"

Oh my goodness. It was like he knew my feelings.

A lone finger skimmed my cheek and played with the ends of my scarf. "I saw your scar heal. Why do you still wear this?"

"Habit." I raised my chin and soaked in the longing on his face.

"Get inside." His gruff voice played hockey with my heart, a back-and-forth tug of war between desire and uncertainty. His mysteriousness fed my yearning for touch, and he'd made me feel in control.

I stalled, basking in this new feeling. "If I turn around, are you going to sink your fangs in my neck?"

He pressed a hard chest against me so I could feel all of him. "Is that what you want?"

Oh heaven. Safe. This was my kind of protection. If I let this go any further, we'd be in bed before too long. I needed to shake off this attraction.

"I never set foot inside your dwelling." Warren pulled back and leaned against the stairway railing, leaving me bereft and wanting.

"What?"

"Keys..." Warren panted. "Your keys... apologizing for keys..." He was not unaffected by desire.

"Oh!" I'd called Diego about the breaking and entering this afternoon to return my car keys.

"I tossed them in..." He made a motion of throwing something at his chest. "They landed on your kitchen counter."

I did not want to contemplate all of that. Instead, I fiddled with my keys, looking toward my neighbor's door. "Can I trust that you won't barge into Thomas's apartment and finish your conversation?"

Warren stilled. "I'm going home after you're safely tucked away on the other side of that door."

"To the island?" How did that work? Was there a bridge or did he hop on a helicopter back home? Or did he pop through himself like a doorway? Or was he going to go through the Rusty Teapot's freezer door like Diego?

"Don't worry." He smiled. "If needed, I'll come quick enough to save you from another disaster."

"Hey! I was fine. No meddling necessary." I unlocked the deadbolt and opened my door.

He narrowed his eyes. "That would require you not bargaining with demons."

I gave him my best deadpan stare. "Except you?"

"I'm serious," he growled. "You have no idea the power you wield."

"Because no one will tell me." I turned to face him.

Warren took a breath and lifted his head as if asking God for mercy. "Fine. I will answer your questions. Tomorrow. It's late."

"All of them?"

"Yes," his answer a snap of impatience.

I felt a tingle, much like the one Thomas said was a bond agreement, snap an anchor within my chest.

A low tiger's growl vibrated. Eyes wild, Warren exposed his jagged teeth. He lifted his arm and pointed to my door and said in garbled speech, "Get inside."

I knew better than to talk back this time. I raced to get inside. Once behind a barrier, I looked through the peephole.

Warren paced at my door.

I said loud enough for him to hear, "Did you feel that? Did we make a bond?"

"Yes." He leaned up against my apartment entry with both hands and a bowed head.

"Are you okay?"

Warren sighed and nodded. "I should have known that was coming."

What do I say to that?

He searched in his pocket and pulled something out and kneeled out of my sight.

"Hey, what are you doing?" I went on my toes to see if I could spot him. No dice. The fish-eyed peephole wasn't any use.

"Keeping you safe." A scraping followed along my door jam.

I did not like the sound of that.

"Don't you dare!" I whipped open my door.

Warren held white chalk in his hands, and he scribbled up the side of my door. It could have been a language, hieroglyphics, or doodles—I didn't care.

"What are you doing?"

His answer was monotone. "I'm writing."

Oh, my goodness in heaven. He had to answer my questions! We'd made a bond. The glee was euphoric!

Warren's nose flared, and the glare of disgust knocked me from the height of my mountain top. If he wasn't free to not answer my questions, that one small freedom lost, then it was my fault. It was me who denied him that right.

Careful of my words, I asked, "May I know why?"

His seething glare softened to a placid annoyance, and he went back to writing on the wall. "It's to keep you safe."

Great. Avoidance tactics.

Warren expanded on his answer. "Anyone trying to enter your domicile will be directed to me. Don't invite people over." He scribbled over the outside molding of my door.

"So, you're making a portal? If they try to walk through this door, it's like call forwarding or something?"

He smirked. "Something like that."

"What if I want a pizza? You gonna deliver it yourself?"

"Yes." Warren pinched his nose and sighed. "Do you want a pizza? I'd rather you stay here."

Ouch. Every question needed an answer. "No. I have food."

He continued scratching chalk letters around my door. "You can leave, and you can come back in, but anyone else will not make it past the threshold. If I was obsessive, I'd do this on your window." He paused and knelt to the floor. "I might be obsessive."

Warren was doing this to protect me. It wasn't like I was trapped. But I couldn't pass this opportunity up. "Warren—" I paused. When you want something for so long, so badly, sometimes the journey becomes more important than the quest.

He raised a hand. "Before you ask, do you really want the answer?"

"Yes." No hesitation. Though, there was some doubt. Even if I ask him about my mother, he will only answer in his demon way. Demons have a way of answering without revealing the truth.

He waited, stopping his scribbling, understanding this was a moment of truth for me. "Where is Eli Florentine?"

Warren's head cocked to the side. "That's not the question you want to ask."

"Yes, it is."

"Tomorrow." He knelt and started writing again. "I said I would answer your questions tomorrow."

"No. I want to know now."

Warren finished encasing my doorframe with swirls and lines, and stood up, throwing the chalk down the hall. He leaned in with every syllable of the word. "To-mor-row." His face was too close.

Frustration made me want to scream, but I held it in and used a different tactic. Honey gathered more flies than... other things.

"No goodnight kiss for you." I stepping as far back as I could while still holding on to the door knob.

"Miles Evans." His sultry cadence rumbled. Warren could match my strategy with whiplash speed.

"Yes?" Was he going to kiss me?

In a low whisper, he asked, "What is your real name?"

I slammed the door so fast it probably grazed his nose. My heart slammed in my chest. Fuuuudge. Of course, he knew my name was fakish. Legally, it was Makayla Evans. A paper trail to throw off anyone looking for me. Chamomile Eirian was my name at birth. Friends called me Miles because it didn't throw me off like being called Makayla.

After a breath and my wits coming back, I readied to face him again and opened the door, but he was gone.

Wonderful.

Still, he wasn't going to stop me from tracking down shadows that could lead me to my mother. Maybe, if the deal with Thomas didn't pan out, Warren could help me after all.

CHAPTER 11

I STAYED UP AS late as possible. Exhaustion pushed away the fear keeping me awake. From all that happened lately, I knew I'd have one of those nightmares. The kind that used my past to haunt my subconscious.

At about 1 a.m., my eyes grew heavy, and my body weighed down all thought until my consciousness sank into the abyss.

Teeth chased me down a dark hall. Hands grabbed at my arms, my waist, and my legs. I tried pulling myself free only for more grasping fingers reaching for me. Arms ripped through the floor, the walls, and the ceiling until the hall became a tunnel of limbs. Teeth replaced fingers.

Sharp, vicious fangs sank into my skin. Lip-shaped puncture wounds riddled my arms and legs. Incisors pierced my stomach. No matter how many nights my nightmare returned, I wasn't used to it.

The same teeth had chased me through the same dark halls of the same Gothic mansion every night since I was twelve. Disjointed memories, teeth, blood, all tumbled in a kaleidoscope of horror.

I screamed to ward off the pain. As I twisted to break free, tearing my skin at the price of freedom, an unnerving inhuman screech echoed down the hall.

Everything stopped.

Silence.

The sickly sound of broken bones and the dripping gore of a set of disembodied arms landed on the floor with a thunk. A thousand screams howled as one. My hands flew to cover my ears. Smoke and heat filtered into the hall of hands. A fierce warning growl of a leopard shook the hallway. One by one, as if pulled from the root and sucked into the ground, the arms with teeth disappeared beyond the black ether.

Chaos erupted. Arms swung wild. Cries wailed. Hands grabbed for me, and I swatted them away, running for the end of the hall. I ran toward a light.

It wasn't far to reach, and I saw a cracked open door. I didn't know where it led to but spent little time thinking about consequences and burst through to my escape.

I slammed the heavy oak door and turned around. A gold-lit room with a fireplace, cushy chairs, and an honest-to-mercy eighteenth-century bed, curtains included, awaited me. The terror was gone. I felt safe. Warm.

I was too exhausted to run, and an empty bed waited for me. My consciousness faded.

IN A LANGUID HAZE, I was acutely aware of my surroundings, the sensation of my body nestled against something warm and inviting. My knees bent, I knew I was sitting up and sank deeper onto the satin skin, a soft mattress cradling my weight, beneath me. It was a bizarre yet intoxicating sensation, as if I had slipped into a surreal world where reality and dreams intertwined. Someone was beneath me, their presence both thrilling and disorienting.

Mind still fogged by the remnants of sleep, I began to rock back and forth, letting the most exquisite pleasure bloom through my core. Each gentle motion ignited a slow-burning fire within me, sending waves of heat cascading through my body. Featherlight touches skimmed my arms—ghostly fingers that traced invisible patterns on my skin, coaxing a sigh of pleasure from my lips. My hands glided over warm, delicious skin, exploring with a lazy curiosity, reveling in the soft contours beneath my fingertips.

A man's low moan split the air, and the sound resonated deep inside me. The vibration of his pleasure sent an intoxicating thrill spiraling into my core. It was primal, raw, awakening every nerve ending to life. Curiosity finally compelled me to open my eyes, and the world sharpened into focus. To my astonishment, Warren's sharp features were illuminated by the soft glow of the firelight filtering through the curtains. There I was, slowly riding him, him inside me, our bodies entwined in a tableau that felt both intimate and wildly inappropriate—like a softer, more erotic version of an R-rated film.

Warren snapped his eyes open, his mouth parting in astonishment.

"Miles Evans?" His voice was heavy with shock, each syllable tinged with a mix of confusion.

You're not the only one stunned, buddy.

Our gazes locked, an electric current passing between us, each of us grappling with the absurdity of the situation. Yet, my hips continued surging, letting pleasure coax me in continuing this sexual dance.

I felt a rush of mischief at the corner of my lips, a smile creeping forth while riding him. "Interesting scene for the subconscious to conjure up," I said, my voice airy, as if we were sharing a private joke amidst the unraveling chaos.

Warren's brow furrowed, caught between incredulity and an undeniable allure that made the air thrum with tension. The absurdity of the scenario hung between us, him beneath me as I rocked, a heavy mist tangled within the crackling firelight. I couldn't help but chuckle softly, the bubble of laughter breaking the spell of silence that swayed around the edges of our unexpected awakening.

"It is you, Miles, yes?" he asked, half serious, half amused, as if daring me to affirm his surreal experience. I recognized a note of concern in his voice, and I didn't want him, or anyone, dream or not, to have an ounce of fear. Not from me.

I leaned close to his ear, my heart pounding. "Easy, big fella, it's me."

"Say your name," he hissed. "Say it."

His alarm broke my heart. If I didn't know this was a dream, I wouldn't be taking this so well either.

"It's me," I said. "Miles Evans. I am Miles Evans."

He relaxed and let out a sigh. "Ah, good. This is okay then."

Oh, so I was allowed, but not just anyone, huh? Didn't that warm a girl's heart.

Warren allowed me to push him to the mattress and moaned. His voice no longer held the previous reservation. His eyelids closed halfway, and he moved his hips in time with mine, seeking to get deeper inside me. He was bare, not only in clothing but also in demeanor. Eyes of desire, lips twitching, caressing hands, hips pushing up seeking how far we could go. He was lost to the whims of my dream, and my heating libido.

"You can feel me through the joining, yes?" he asked.

"Mmmm... here, right?" I touched just below my navel. My hips rolled, and in a hazy grasp for reality, I thought, This is just a dream.

"You like that?" I teased, my voice a sultry whisper, the boundaries of reality blurring in that tantalizing moment. The warmth of his skin against mine sent shivers racing down my spine—and I couldn't help but think, Is this more than a dream?

The absurdity deepened as he lay there, tangled up in a web of emotions I didn't fully understand. Warren was sexy in a terrifying way. His penchant for protection was a subliminal message. My mind was trying to tell me I could trust him. The jury was still out though.

A connection webbed through my blood, thrumming like a live wire beneath my skin. In that moment, I became part of a whole, an intertwining of desires that electrified the air around us. It was deliciously forbidden, a thrill that ignited every nerve ending. The beauty of it swept over me like a warm tide, the kind that pulled me under and left me gasping for breath but craving more of its depths.

With intent, I leaned over him, my breath mingling with his, my heart racing with the power of the moment. I pressed his hands against the mattress, pinning him down with an authority that both startled and exhilarated me. Silk sheets crumpled beneath him, echoing the tension that hung between us. Our eyes locked, a silent battle of wills beneath the surface. I could feel his pulse quickening beneath my touch, a primal rhythm that matched the one racing in my chest.

"Do you want this?" I whispered into his face, my voice low and sultry, laced with the promise of all that was to come. I lorded my control over him, but he seemed powerless under my spell. The air was thick, heavy with unspoken words and raw longing.

Warren arched his back, a shiver running through him as he surrendered to the sensation. A toe-curling moan escaped his lips—deep and resonant, the kind of deep sound only a man with a voice that could both command and beg could manage.

Wow. Deprived much?

Each sound he made fueled the fire within me, and as he writhed beneath my grip, I felt myself drawn further into the delicious chaos of it all. I was both in control and utterly lost, a dizzying paradox that sent my heart racing.

With gritted teeth, he strained against the constraints of my measly hold, a fierce determination shadowing his features.

"Take what you need, quickly. I won't last," he urged, his voice a low rumble that seemed to vibrate through the very essence of the room.

Urgency accompanied his words, an intoxicating blend of need and desperation that urged me forward, yet the challenge lingered in the air. How could I possibly move quickly when every ounce of me wanted to savor this moment, to prolong this exquisite dance?

The world outside ceased to exist. It was just the two of us, wrapped in a cocoon of tension and desire. Every heartbeat echoed in my ears like a drum, setting the rhythm for what was to come. I leaned in closer, my lips nearly grazing his ear as I embraced the intoxicating power I held over him, my heart thrumming in harmony with the unyielding passion that pulled us together like gravity.

In that breathless moment, I understood this was more than a mere connection—it was a call to explore the labyrinth of our forbidden needs and hidden truths. Bound by the thrill of surrender and strength, we were two forces colliding, ready to ignite the night.

He tried moving his hands, but I used them for leverage in rolling my hips, tormenting him with a rhythm that seemed to push him right to the edge of madness. The intensity between us crackled like electricity, sending jolts of pleasure coursing through my body. He bucked beneath me, grunting and frenzied, desperate, primal—each thrust was a plea for more, for faster, for deeper. I held my ground, a teasing smile playing on my lips as I denied him, savoring the power I had over him in this moment.

Eyes wild and panting, I could see the raw desperation flickering in his gaze, a silent battle raging within him. He was so close—I could practically taste it— to that moment when he would completely lose himself in the euphoria. Just as I anticipated the frantic crescendo of his desire, I tightened my grip on his hands, prolonging the delicious tension that hung between us. Only in dreams could I hold him back like this, and the thrill was intoxicating.

Warren struggled against my grasp, his breath coming in ragged bursts as he called my name. "Miles..." The way he said it—a mix of frustration and yearning—sent a thrill down my spine. His plea was an empowering anthem, promising dark pleasures that lay just beyond the edge of restraint. It was a challenge, an invitation wrapped in need, beckoning me deeper into this beautifully chaotic dance.

His breath mingled with mine, the urgency in his movements mirrored in the rhythm of my heart, each beat a testament to the fire burning between us. I surrendered to the wave of sensation, letting go of my calculated control. The room spun around us, consumed by the power of our bodies locked together in this raw, primal embrace.

The anticipation, the urgency, the desperation—it all coalesced into a symphony of pleasure and possession. I relished the pulse of his desire matching my own, each thrust igniting every nerve ending in my body. This was more than just a physical connection. It was an exploration of our limits, a journey through passion that propelled us both to the edge of ecstasy. And I knew, at that moment, we were both lost to the world—this dream—bound in an unbreakable rhythm of pleasure, each movement a step further into blissful oblivion.

When I finally relented, allowing him the freedom of his hands, he clamped down on my hips with newfound intensity. A triumphant roar echoed off the walls of the room, a sound that reverberated through my core. Warren drove deeper, claiming me, marking me with his ferocity. I could feel him expand inside me, stretching me utterly, the sensation of him filling me almost overwhelming...

I sat up in my own apartment, in my own bed, alone. The echo of a desperate howl died as the familiarity of my home came to focus.

A dream. Only a dream. One that left my thighs slick, my core aching, and altered my perception of a terrifying demon. But that wasn't Warren. It was a fantasy of him. It took my breath away and left me with euphoric liberation.

Sexually, I'd been left high and dry.

While I was checking the time on my phone, an unknown call started vibrating my cell. Ugh. Didn't everyone know I was on vacay for the next few weeks? Should I answer? It was the middle of the night, but to most of my clientele, this was like midday to them.

"Hello?" I answered.

Heavy breathing on the line roiled my temper. I would have hung up, but the familiar hiss and crack of a fire in the background gave me pause. Before I could give whoever a piece of my mind, a raspy voice huffed, "Miles Evans."

The voice, smooth as Texas whiskey with hints of smokey innuendo, could only be that of one demon.

"Warren." I tried to play it cool, but my voice broke. "What do you want?"

"Oh no, my little morsel, it's not what I want, but what I can give you." His smile came through even over the phone.

Shock. Disbelief. Silence. He was flirting with me. Deliciously. This tightly wound loose cannon of a demon wanted to play. It was so far off his usual demeanor that I didn't know what to say.

It didn't matter. He kept talking.

"Let me sate your need, little one."

My mouth watered. My insides quivered.

"Yes, little one," he purred. "Let me take care of you."

His offer was tempting, but a demon was still dangerous no matter what they promised.

"I know you are cautious, Miles. Tie me to your bed if need be. I'll bring parachute cord. Anything you need to feel safe."

"You'd let me tie you up?"

"Mmmm, it would set you free to know I could not move, correct?"

Huh? "When?" That snapped me out of the sexual haze. "Wait, what are you talking about?"

"We are connected, Miles. Much to my dismay."

"When have I ever made you immobile?"

"I have already explained this." A patient sigh crackled over the line. "I'm not playing this game, Miles or whatever your name is."

"Don't you have to answer my questions?"

A pause, then Warren said, "The bond only goes one way with you, does it? What else was I expecting from a blood doll."

There was the stiff, bullish devil I was used to. "Don't blame me. I asked. You answered."

"And I'm a fool for allowing you to play both sides."

"What does that mean, Warren?"

"Are you that thickheaded, or are you playing dumb for a reason? Fine. You want an answer? How is this one. We. Are. Connected. That means when you have a nightmare, it affects me. When you want to play out your sexual fantasies, it affects me. When you tether yourself to one of the lowest possible denominators, it affects me."

It took me a moment to process. That was him in my dream. The real Warren. I rode him like a starlet trying to convince a famous director to be cast in his blockbuster movie. I voiced the thought playing over in my mind. "I was expecting a demon to last a little longer."

He huffed. "Really, Miles? Dick jokes? How childish."

Neither of us spoke until he cleared his throat, and said, with a sarcastic note, "I apologize for disturbing you."

Warren putting distance between us didn't sit well. "Wait! Please, I want to confirm…" I could scarcely talk about my nightmares, and my voice lowered to a whisper. "You were the thing that scared away the arms with teeth?"

"Mmmm… that was a particularly nasty nightmare."

Coming from the biggest badass I'd ever met, that was saying something. "You were in my dream with me? Is that what you mean when you say we're connected?"

A relieved sigh tickled in my ear. "There's too much to explain, and I don't want to do this right now."

"You're the one who called." And busted into my dream, though, to be fair, I was glad he had.

A groan turned into a swishing that sounded like he was setting himself on bed sheets. A flash of silk linens heated my imagination and my cheeks.

"In short, we are bonded. That means I felt that spark of heat in you that just occurred."

My stomach dropped. He can read minds?

"And your clenched middle is exactly the reaction I'm trying to avoid," he said.

"Are you telepathic?"

Another groan. "It's your blood, Miles. I know what you're feeling because I happen to still have a healthy dose of your blood in my system."

Hold on. "You feel what I feel?"

"I don't always know what you're thinking, but yes. I feel what you feel."

"Is that why you came in like a dark horse, slammed Thomas through a portal, and scared him off when I met him in the hallway?"

"Not only were you terrified both times, but I felt you enter a contract, and I had no clue as to the arrangement or with whom. That would bring any demon to insanity."

"Why didn't you explain this to me earlier?"

His groan turned into a tiger's growl. This time, his inhuman snarl didn't scare me and touched places below my waistline.

"I have been told I am more amenable after being satiated, sexually and sustainably."

"You didn't explain this to me because you were hangry?" Ply him with food—or in this case, blood and sex—and he talks. Got it.

"If I remain connected to you, that means I am also responsible for you. You've already seen how I react to your fear. What would I do for your safety? You're angry?"

"How you act is not my responsibility."

"I would in time adjust to your flightiness."

"Hey!"

"But I have decided to let the blood-bond fade," he mumbled, "just in case."

I snorted, trying to hide my hurt. "Well, buddy, I don't want you to feel my feelings either."

"It's for the best, Miles."

"Just in case you catch emotions or something?"

"No." His voice went cold. "Just in case you do turn out to be like most blood dolls."

The connotation in his words set me off. "Screw. You. If you can feel me, feel my intentions, then screw you if you think I'll become some monster. And if you think I might, then why not help me out, huh? Why not guide me? Why not steer me in the right direction?"

"You don't know what you're asking."

"For help? Jiminy Crickets, Warren, do you know how long I've been alone? Stumbling in the dark? Trying to make it from day to day? Do you know how hard it is asking for help, from anyone?"

"I wouldn't be the best candidate to help you in your endeavors. Yes, I know you're hiding something. I know you're struggling. And yet, you're asking me to show you the way out?"

"Can't be hard. I'll do the opposite of what you'd do," I sneered.

"Miles Evans, or whatever your name is, choose your path wisely. Because if you go wrong, it will be me coming after you."

Chapter 12

WARREN CORONER WAS THE biggest jerk-face I'd ever met. After his connotation he'd end my life if I became evil, I hit the End button on the call. Then I powered my phone off. I felt no satisfaction in pushing a button. Raising my hand, I flung my phone across my single-room apartment. Plastic met wall with a crack, and my cell clattered to the floor. The phone didn't survive my outrage.

I'd show him. If I hadn't turned evil by now, with everything that happened to me, then he didn't know a damn thing about me. The nerve of that guy. It made me want to shake him and ask, What's wrong with you?

I was entirely awake now. Good thing the Rusty Teapot was open. I put on a pair of jeans and a secondhand T-shirt, finishing off the ensemble with a scarf, though there were no fresh holes in my neck, which was nice, but still reminded me of Warren jerk-face Coroner.

The fish lens showed an empty hall. I threw my door open and cautiously stepped beyond the threshold of my apartment. A voice called my name as soon as the deadbolt clanked.

"Miles?"

I jumped and turned around.

Thomas's blue eye peeked through a a narrow sliver of his door.

"Holy moly. Don't scare me like that." I shut down the spike of terror that ran through me, knowing Warren would feel it. If he showed up now, I would slap him.

When my vampire neighbor didn't say anything, I shoved my annoyance at Thomas, unable to curb rising bubbles of resentment, and asked, "What?"

He still didn't say anything and stared at me like I was a three-headed dog. I had other questions, but not enough patience to ask them. Since Thomas wasn't talking, I turned for the stairs.

"Is my help not useful?" Thomas said.

"Huh?" I turned, trying to understand his question. Vampires could be so weird sometimes. "Your help? You mean answering my questions?"

His eye searched the hall.

"He's not here," I said.

Thomas opened the door a little wider, so I could see both of his eyes. "Are you all right?"

"Why do you care?" Whoa. The words left my mouth before I could stop them. "I'm sorry..."

"What if I wanted to petition to become part of your enclave?" Thomas opened his door wider exposing a dark hall. "Then I would care a lot."

I rolled my eyes. "I don't have an enclave."

"Yes. You do. You might not think of them as such, but the people you call clients, those humans, they are your enclave. Having me at your side, despite what Warren says, legitimizes it."

"Don't talk to me about him." I blanched.

He cocked his head. "Is your enforcer giving you a hard time?"

"He's not my anything."

Thomas ventured further out. "Where are you going?"

"Rusty Teapot," I said, yawning.

"Wonderful." He stood next to me in the blink of an eye. His door closed. The Dracule stood there, waiting, face as eager as a golden retriever.

I couldn't help but smile. "Would you like to go with me?"

He nodded and followed me down the stairs.

The Rusty Teapot was in a lull before the morning rush, and we sat in the booth by the window watching the sun rise. Sunlight crept up his arm as Dolores took our order. Juice for me, coffee for Thomas. Before the bright rays stretched their arms of light over the city, Thomas pulled the shade down, covering the window.

We sat in silence until juice, coffee, and a plate piled high with pancakes hit the table. Thomas watched me as he sipped his own cup of joe. But finally, he spoke.

"You have the power to claim territory," he said, wrapping his hands around a white ceramic mug. "But you don't have political influence. Yet." He leaned forward over his coffee, as if the drink gave him tribute.

"Why would I need that?" I shoved a pancake into my mouth.

He sighed and shook his head. "To give you the information you want."

Tempting. I waited for him to continue. He sipped at his coffee.

"I'm not a mind reader, Thomas."

"And I'm going out on a limb, here. Especially since Warren made our contract null."

I winced. "Sorry. I didn't know he was going to show up and squeeze the life out of you."

Thomas snorted. "Yeah, well, God's fucking favorite can do what he wants."

His comment made me slow down on my pancake intake. "God's favorite?"

He shrugged. "It's a rumor."

Did that mean Warren was an angel? Good thing a pancake stayed my words. The things I wanted to say to God might get me struck with lightning.

"What rumor?" I put down my fork and sat back awaiting his answer.

Thomas sighed. "Perhaps you'll want to ask Warren."

"No. Wait. Why did you call him Adam's son? Adam who?"

A smug smile spread across his handsome face. "Have you read the Bible, Miles?"

"The Bible... do you mean Adam like the Garden of Eden Adam?" I gaped at Thomas.

People started filtering in for breakfast. The weird thing was that the booth behind me and the one in front of me remained empty.

Thomas leaned back. He ignored my question and said, "If I become part of your enclave, I could bring you the missing pieces you need to protect yourself and the clique. I might even answer your question about Warren."

Aside from not fully comprehending what the missing pieces were, I knew there was more to Thomas than his giving nature. "What do you get in return?"

He licked his lips and smiled. "You."

There it was. Thomas wanted a reliable meal. I couldn't blame him.

"You want in my enclave even though Warren is in it?"

"If we were both in your circle, we wouldn't be at odds. No matter what he says, he wouldn't touch me once I was connected to you."

"I'll think about it." It might be worth having Thomas drink my blood to keep them both from killing each other. Then again, if he knew I was a blood doll, he might offer me the deal I couldn't refuse. But maybe Warren would help me keep my autonomy. No, I needed to stop thinking about jerk-face Warren.

Right as my pancakes were digesting, Lilly came bouncing into the cozy diner. She spotted me and made a beeline for our table. Her slink-tight dress was a black number with lace covering her arms and neckline.

When she stepped up to our table, I smiled bright. "Wow, what high-powered lawyer are you seducing today?"

She chuckled. "You are too sweet. I was checking in. Will you be around tonight?"

"I think so." But if Eustachys's information panned out, then I could be on the run with my mom. "Why?"

"Good." Lilly turned to Thomas. "Who's this?" Her flirty tone came out more like a challenge.

"Lil, this is Thomas," I introduced. "You can talk. He's safe." In the sense that he knew I was a donor.

Everyone was careful about the scene. Some flaunted that they were "vampires" but kept the circle safe from people who didn't understand our way.

Thomas stared up at her with big round eyes and a half-gapping mouth. I expected him to be all over her with his charm and wit. She was gorgeous and totally loved being seen.

"Done with Warren already, huh?"

"How do you even know about him?" I bemoaned.

"Word gets around. You think I wouldn't know about that big scene at Cuppa Shot?"

"Ugh! I don't want to talk about that jerk-face," I huffed.

A slow smile crept up her face. "I don't know. Sounds like you two were hitting it off."

"I don't want to hear his name right now." I melted over the table and covered my head with my arms.

She laughed. "Trouble in paradise?"

"More like match made in hell. I blame you, by the way."

Lilly leaned to one side and dropped her amusement. "You give the word. If he doesn't treat you right, I will sing him a song he won't wake from."

I snorted. Like she could do anything to him, but the sentiment was nice. "Don't bother." I'd already been on the Warren murder ride—and all I got was a lousy T-shirt.

Plus, his words were an empty threat. He'd come to save me, twice. Both times were without me asking. Yes, he blew things way out of proportion, but no one was perfect. He went out of his way to see me safe. Warren was also the only demon that knew what I was and didn't propose to take away my freedom. He'd see I wasn't a threat to anyone.

"Well, okay but the offer still stands." Lilly swept her red hair over her shoulder. "Men need to be put in their place every so often."

That was Lil. A bit of a harsh feminist.

"Nice to meet you, Thomas." Lilly waved and walked with purpose out of the Rusty Teapot.

Thomas shrank in a subdued quiet and consoled his coffee mug like it was his best friend.

"You okay?" I asked.

"Yeah…" He smiled. "Yeah." He nodded. More like he was trying to convince himself of his own words.

"Well, I'm on my way downtown." I scooted to the end of the booth.

Thomas paused, like he was thinking, then swung his best smile to me. "Great, I can tag along."

"Uhhh…" I paused. "Sorry, bud, but this is personal."

Thomas scowled. "My name is not Bud."

"Nonetheless, you aren't going with me." I stood at the end of our table.

He grabbed the bill Dolores set down on the table and followed me to the cash register.

"Miles, I'm a vampire. I know when someone's going to do sketchy shit."

"You mean you're a Dracule, right?" I was rather pleased that I could toss info around. See, I'm not a total noob.

Thomas laughed. "Only royalty cares about stuffy formalities least they be shuffled in with the commoners." He handed a large bill to the cashier and waived off the change. "I guess Warren is where you're getting your insight."

I started pulling out my own wallet. "Warren is considered royalty? Like a prince or something?"

Thomas waved off the credit card I tried giving to the cashier. "That's fairly accurate. You could call him the first prince."

"First prince?" I choked. "Like the first dark prince? As in the devil?"

Thomas wheezed and then laughed. "As in the first prince in the history of man."

"Oh-kay." I couldn't even comprehend that.

I put my wallet away and sighed against the gnawing guilt for giving in and allowing him to pay for breakfast.

"So... downtown." He lifted his elbow in invitation for me to wrap my hand around it.

I didn't take his offered arm and headed to the exit. "I guess I can't stop you from following."

"Miles, I want to keep you safe."

"Because I'm a possible meal?"

Thomas took a moment to answer. "Because you're wandering deeper in a world that will literally eat you alive. I like you," he whispered. "I don't want to see those close to me hurt."

I scrutinized his face, scanning for exaggeration or an underlying meaning.

"And I do admit..." he said with a grin, chasing the worry away from his face. "I want a taste of you. If I stick around, maybe I'll be rewarded." Thomas wiggled his eyebrows and licked his lips.

Yep. Always the ulterior motive. "Dream on," I teased.

"Are your fees exorbitant or are you no longer donating?"

"Haven't decided."

WE KEPT UP THE banter while I drove us downtown. His hands were animation in motion as he talked in the passenger seat. "Say there is a situation. What do you want me to do?"

"A situation?" I mused. Both times he'd come against Warren, he'd been as effective as a kitten.

"I'm not weak!" He'd blasted my right ear with an inhuman screech. The intensity of his stare could have scalded my brain. His face grew red with anger.

"Okay," I said softly. My shoulders went stiff. That's right, Miles, he's a vampire. Treat him accordingly.

Thomas sighed, sat straight, and looked out the windshield. "Granted I'm no match for the echelon, but I can protect you from anything else."

I had to be careful and choose my words. It was madness to let my guard down around him, but he'd been so humanlike, so normal, I'd forgotten myself.

"If a need arises, I would..." What was the right word here? If I said "appreciate," it would connote a reward. "Grateful" was even worse.

"Yes or no, Miles," Thomas said. "Don't overthink."

"Don't expect a reward from me." I gave him a disapproving side-eye.

"Your safety is all the thanks I need." He grinned with blocky teeth.

"Sure, sure..."

He kept asking me, in different ways, to become a part of my enclave. My answers were always noncommittal. I parked my car along a side street and made my way to the alley where Eustachys showed me the video anomaly. Thomas didn't say a word once we got out of the car and scanned the area with a critical eye.

It was before the morning rush when the air remained cool and damp. People would soon fill the streets on their way to work and school. Downtown's quirky buildings and hidden alleyways loomed in warning. I walked to the alcove, where I'd seen Military Jacket guy bolt inhumanly fast from the sidewalk to the alleyway, and started down the narrow path. Thomas lagged behind.

Brick walls loomed around me, their cold, rough surfaces providing no hints or whispers of where Military Jacket guy had gone. A dumpster, grimy and half hidden by overflowing trash, sat like a reluctant sentinel. I kicked aside a crumpled soda can, exasperated, glancing again at the two buildings that stood side by side—stoic and silent, devoid of doors, windows, fire escapes, or any sign of life.

I felt like a moth drawn to an unseen flame, captivated yet thwarted by the oppressive atmosphere. There had to be a way in, a clue left unnoticed, but as I inspected the inky crevices and shadows, nothing emerged. A faint sound echoed in the distance, but it was swallowed by the heavy silence that clung to the alley like a thick fog.

With a sigh, I retraced my steps, Thomas behind me, each crunch of glass beneath my shoes a reminder of the isolation from the busy streets at both ends of the passage. I ventured slowly along the alley, scanning for any anomalies in the grimy bricks. Some wore the scars of age and neglect, others were mottled with graffiti, but none revealed the path that Military Jacket guy had taken.

Turning sharply, I maneuvered around the dumpster, its foul stench mixing with the musty aroma of decay. I leaned against the rough brick, pushing my fingers into the jagged surface as if my touch could unveil something hidden. The huge bulk of the buildings loomed closer, leaving me feeling like a minor character in a story far too grand for my plight.

Determined, I stepped back and surveyed the whole view. Even though the alley was a straight path between these buildings, both structures seemed purposefully constructed to obfuscate. My eyes traced the contours of the brickwork, searching for any subtle variations—a loose stone, a crack deep enough to hide a secret. Footholds to the roof, anything.

Yes, Military Jacket guy could have used this alleyway as a shortcut through to the other side, but Eustachys seemed sure he hadn't. He knew who he was looking for and didn't seem as affected by the trick of light. I trusted the PI's gut feeling.

It was then that I noticed a barely perceptible groove running diagonally across one wall, shadowy and mysterious. My heart raced as I approached, feeling a tingling sensation in my fingertips. Could this be the trace of a hidden door? I pressed my palm against it, letting my weight lean into the wall. Beneath my touch, the brick felt uneven, as if it might shift if coaxed just right.

Suddenly, from deep within my mind, a memory flickered to life—a whispered story of hidden entrances and long-lost passages found only by those who dared to seek. I needed to find out if this was merely a figment of my hope or a real chance to pursue Military Jacket guy.

I stepped back, studying the wall from different angles, my thoughts a whirlwind of possibilities. If a hidden entrance existed here, it needed a keystone—something that would activate its release. I dug through my pockets, searching for anything I could use. A stick, a small rock, anything to prod or poke at the potential passage. I found a pen and pulled it out. This would do the trick.

With my heart pounding and anticipation electrifying the air around me, I took a deep breath and pressed the pen against the groove, pushing harder.

The pen broke, and the last vestiges of my hope snapped along with it.

"Of course." Another dead end. It felt like I was so close. Like I had something with Eustachys's video, and this was going to be my big break. I threw the broken pen down and kicked at the wall, frustrated.

"Not what you were looking for?" Thomas strolled up with his hands in his pockets.

"Not at all." I started walking toward the light, wanting to get away from the shadowed alleyway and the uncomfortable air.

"Maybe, if you tell me what you're looking for, I could help."

Ha. If he only knew. There would be no going back if I told him the whole story. He might ask questions which could lead him to finding out I was a blood doll. He already knew more than I was comfortable with. I didn't expect Thomas to be as benevolent as Warren, allowing me freedom instead of the offer I couldn't refuse. Warren's benevolence afforded him my gratitude, and a small measure of trust. Thomas, not so much.

I made my way to sunlight, stepped out of the alley's gloom, and slumped my back against the sun-heated wall. I watched traffic go by, feeling defeated. The brick felt unmovable. Hard. Unyielding. Warm. Stable. Something I'd never had in my life.

The screech of bus brakes and the smell of diesel brought my thoughts to the outside world.

"Miles?" Thomas shifted his eyes, looking down the alleyway. "We should go."

I'd kept things hidden for both my mom's and protection and my own. I'd been trying to do this alone, and so far, I was coming up with zilch. It might be time to extend myself beyond my comfort level. "Hey, Thomas, you remember when we talked, and I told you about my past?"

He grimaced. "I remember."

"There was someone there that helped me escape." I wiped away frustrated tears. "I want to get them out too."

He nodded. "Okay."

"I thought this might be the place, but it's just two buildings..." Big fat tears leaked down my cheeks.

"Shhh..." Thomas wrapped a hand around the back of my head and pulled me close. "No waterworks."

It had been a long time since someone held me without staring at my neck or right before they chomped on my throat. My body stiffened, conditionally ready for pain, but Thomas soothed my nerves as he glided a hand up and down my back. It wasn't sexual, but there was an intimacy in the motion. For a guilty moment, I allowed him to stroke my back and try to calm me.

"This person is important to you." His voice wavered as if he were in pain. "We can find them." He looked down both sidewalks. "But here in this busy street might not be the best place. Let's go back."

"Yeah, sure." I followed him as the streets filled with cars, and people filtered onto the footpath. He held my hand, guiding me through the crowd, away from the alley, as I stared off into nothing.

Out of all the sounds of the city—people walking, cars passing by, and the squeal of bus brakes—I heard the determined strides and familiar heels striking the ground. It was as if all the noise around me were muffled, but those footfalls were sharp and focused. I turned to watch Lilly, in her black lace get up and high-powered shoes, step from the street to the sidewalk and into the alley. The same alley spanning between the two buildings with no doors. I blinked, and she was gone. She hadn't seen me through the throng of people on the move.

I pulled away from Thomas and called out, "Lilly?"

Thomas jerked his head, swiveling his neck, and on the lookout.

The crowd pushed me back, like I was a trout swimming upstream, but I knew who I had seen. What was she doing here? I bolted past the crowd, swerving and twisting, dodging and pushing against bodies to get back to the alleyway. When I got to the mouth, it was empty. I knew she couldn't have walked down that alley in the time it took me to get there.

The entrance was here.

"Miles?" Thomas effortlessly followed. "What are you doing?"

"My friend..." I whispered. A chill ran down my spine. Damn it, I'd seen her plain as day walk into this alley. She didn't melt into a wall.

I began to look at the two buildings. Truly look. They had no fire escapes, no windows, and no doors in the alleyway. I peeked my head around to the side facing the street. I didn't see any doors, windows, or fire escapes on that side facing where most people would enter a building.

"Wait... Miles..." He splayed himself, blocking my path. "I know you want to find your... person you're looking for, but—"

A nagging alarm went off in my head. "Thomas, don't you think it's strange that both these buildings don't have doors, windows or anything to let people in on the two sides where it's most convenient?"

Thomas stared at me without expression—and his nonreaction was the tip-off. Vampires imitate life. Imitate it. This "poker face" of his, the cool undertone as he stared at me might as well have been a scream. I'd caught him off guard. He was calculating how to answer.

"Outta my way." I slipped past him and touched the rough bricks.

He followed me down the alley. "Miles, please, we can figure this out."

That's what I was counting on. I jogged down the length of the narrow path letting my fingers trace the building. Rough mortar and brick wore away at my finger pads.

"There's nothing here." Thomas threw his hands up.

He knew something, but he wasn't going to tell me what it was, so I'd have to trick him into giving me answers.

I turned around, and instead of watching where I was going, I watched the Dracule as I slid down the alley with my fingers gliding along the brick wall. My slow backward steps didn't make him react until...

"What are you doing?" Thomas feigned relaxation. Hard to spot because it was easy for a creature like him to act like he was calm when stoic and emotionless was their usual state.

I was on the right track. I moved to the other building and watched his face. Vampires had "tells" like humans playing poker. Their tells were different, like forgetting to breathe, flashing canines, letting the demon swim too close to their skin, or staring without expression. Thomas was good, but his "tell" was silence, as if holding his breath, before he tried to distract me with his voice.

"Miles, we tried, but it's time to go home and regroup."

My fingers traced over the slightest smooth spot. I circled a single brick with my finger watching Thomas's face.

Our gaze locked. The fear in his eyes was never for himself. Thomas focused on my finger, holding his breath again, and his face went slack.

"Don't," he whispered.

I pushed against the wall and, at first, nothing happened. Then, a single brick sank like it was being held by mud. It slid back so far it looked like the wall would need repairs. A "click" of mechanical gears began to whir. Reminiscent of a scene from a conspiracy movie, part of the wall sank deeper, revealing the outline of a jagged door. Brick scraped against concrete until the slab door detached from the rest of the wall. Another click sounded, and the door slid to the right, revealing a dark opening beyond.

Air whooshed out of the hole, and the inky-black entrance in front of me beckoned. I couldn't see anything, like a veil shielding the inside.

Thomas's chest gently bumped my back. "Don't go in there."

My body shook with the fear of standing in the presence of the unknown. Self-preservation agreed with Thomas's words. My body obeyed his command.

"Stand still. Let the door close. Then let's go home."

Staring into the hole was like coming face-to-face with nothingness. As if anything, or anyone, that walked in there would cease to be.

Life had taught me to ignore self-preservation because my mission wasn't to survive. It was to save my mom. Lilly could also be in there. What if she needed my help?

The clank of gears churned, signaling the door was about to close. Willpower alone lifted my right foot, and momentum carried me through the dark barrier.

CHAPTER 13

AS I STEPPED THROUGH, the wall grated against concrete. Thomas swore and jumped after me just before the door clicked closed.

Darkness gave way to a warm light outlining a brass bar top that spread from one end of the room to the other. Wine bottles filled the shelves behind an illuminated male silhouette wiping glass tumblers. From what I could see, he had short blond hair and wore a suit vest over a clean, white shirt. Nothing about his shadow gave away his identity, but the small hairs along my arms vibrated.

Plush booths lined the walls. Wood tables and chairs blocked a straight path from me to the bar. A stairway went up off to my right. Shadows rose up one by one, surrounding us. Childhood memories pushed a flood of adrenaline in my system.

The bartender inhaled as if he could taste my blood, and said, "Hello, Chamomile. I hear you've been looking for me."

Eli Florentine. The vampire Dracule demon that had kept me in a cage for half my formative young life.

I gave a nervous glance at Thomas. He stood beside me, staring straight ahead with the intensity of a condemned man. My eyes adjusted enough for me to make out Eli's smile.

Breathe. Calm down. The last thing I needed was Warren crashing this party. My mom was here. I could feel it. Knowing his distaste for blood dolls, I couldn't risk the chance Warren might decide we were too dangerous to live before I could get her out.

I looked for exits, things I could use as weapons, even a fire alarm. We were fresh out of luck.

Eli turned his souring face to Thomas. "Welcome home, brother."

My neighbor closed his eyes as I connected the dots. Thomas Florentine. No wonder I was terrified the first time I saw his face. My subconscious recognized him.

"You knew." I turned and scowled at Thomas. "You knew who I was all this time."

Thomas breathed in and sighed with his eyes closed. "I never—"

"Not only that," Eli chuckled. "But he was the last Florentine to see you on your way out. I believe he gave you those supplies."

He meant the bag of things that had been tossed out the window when my mother made for my escape. Thomas was the one to give me the sack. All this time, I thought it'd been Eli who showed me that tiny bit of mercy.

Thomas shot an intensely dangerous glare at his brother. "I never wanted you hurt, Miles."

Eli scoffed. "Hurt? But this was your plan, wasn't it? Or was Pepper taking advantage of the situation?"

Thomas gritted his teeth.

A small figure stepped out from the shadows. She was the same as I remembered her. My mother, Pepper Eirian, swiped her silky raven hair over her shoulder and flashed her brilliant blue eyes at me. "I don't regret it."

She looked stunning with her pale skin in a spaghetti-strap black dress that reached the floor. A genuine smile rested awkwardly on her wary expression, as if she were only half happy to see me. My heart hurt. If I could change reuniting with my mom, it wouldn't be with a crowd of vampires circling us.

"Hello, Mother." I dipped my head. My brain was catching up to reality. My mom was right there. I needed to grab her and run.

"Hello, daughter." She took a step forward.

Eli slid himself out from the bar, by way of a retractable section of countertop and blocked her path.

Pepper's features turned murderous. "What do you think I would do with the lot of you here?" She side-stepped him.

Eli turned, grabbed her forearm, and said, "Wait."

Mother tossed a hand in my direction. "She doesn't even have a proper enclave. She's no threat."

Eli scowled at my mother with an incredulous glower. "I don't think it wise, my Liebling—"

"Wise?" Pepper raised her voice.

The people-shaped shadows edged closer, and I noticed Thomas had a hand in his side coat pocket.

"What is your intention, Chamomile?" Eli held my mom at arm's length.

My intention was to get us out of here.

Our circle grew smaller, and I stepped closer to Thomas. If he helped me escape once, he might help me again. Who knew what his motives were?

"Don't patronize me, Eli," Pepper said. "Don't turn things around." She flashed her blue eyes over me. "They're worried for you, and with good reason." She turned back to Eli. "Still, she's my daughter. I get to do with her as I see fit."

"Consider her worth, my Liebling, before you do anything rash." Eli's shoulders climbed toward his ears.

Thomas crowded my space and hissed a warning at the approaching shadows. The shadows loomed. They were close enough to pounce. Their bodies crouched, my nerves splayed, and trusting Thomas, a lying Dracule, brought no comfort.

Pepper turned her attention to the pack of vampires drawing closer to me, and snarled, "Get back, you greedy heels. Don't think I can't see you edging closer, traitors!"

"Liebling..." Eli said in a gentle tone.

My mother's face twisted in a sneer, looking as beautiful as ever, and pointed an angry finger to the floor. "Kneel!"

Eli, the shadows around us, every Dracule in the room, all of them crouched to the ground, except for Thomas, who grunted and trembled. He'd locked himself in place, but his legs shook, and he looked ready to keel over.

Mother eyed my neighbor and slowly skirted around Eli as if she had all the time in the universe.

"Liebling..." Eli craned his neck to watch her, but she ignored him.

Mother approached Thomas and caressed his cheek, her face wistful. "You were never mine, was I, second of the Florentine, were you?"

Thomas held his ground, but he was fighting to stand. He struggled, breathing in bursts, panting in effort.

She combed his hair back and swatted the side of his face in a playful gesture. "Bad boy."

Mother turned and assessed me. Her eyes landed on my neck. She lifted her hand and traced slim fingers along my scarf. "You've been allowing those Normans to gnaw on you?"

"I'm okay." I scrambled to take off my wrap and showed her my smooth skin underneath. "See? I'm okay." In return, I noticed her scars were light and hardly noticeable.

Being so close to her was more than I could take. I lunged, taking her whole body in a bear hug, and squeezed, intending to never let her go.

Shouts, hisses, and commotion broke out around me, but I didn't care. I had my mom. Tears flowed, and wracking sobs blocked out the noise. Pepper stiffened, and her arms flailed momentarily before she relaxed and wrapped me in a glorious hug.

Mother laughed with a genuine, hearty sound.

"You lot," she said to the group of Dracules with more force than I thought her capable. "Pipe down. She's not attacking me."

What the hell? I would never attack my mother. When I looked over her shoulder, Eli struggled to move, fighting an invisible foe with fangs out, claws extended. His lips wrinkled in a snarl like he'd bleed me dry if he could.

"Come on." I pulled out of our hug and tugged at her wrist. "This is our chance."

Mother pinched her features in confusion. "Our chance?"

"To escape," I whispered.

She looked at me like I'd lost my mind.

"We can do it!" I tugged her toward the door. If I could get in, I could find a way out.

"You want me to go with you, where?" She followed with resistance, but I was larger and managed to pull her a few inches to the door.

"Anywhere but here." I looked at Thomas.

His neck craned to see us out of the corner of his eye. "Miles—"

Mother spun to him. "Shut up!"

Thomas gritted his teeth like he'd taken a blow as he slowly went down on one knee. "Mile... Mi... mmm..."

Wait. Something wasn't right. I looked over at the Dracules. They were staring at me like I was a threat, but they remained kneeling. Eli barred his fangs at me like he wanted to rip out my throat. Some invisible force kept them in place. Even Thomas couldn't move. What was going on? They should be grabbing me, trying to pull us back into our cages like they did when I was twelve.

Pepper yanked out of my hold. "This is my enclave. I'm not letting you have it."

My mouth dropped open. "I'm trying to save you!"

"From what?" She now directed her anger toward me.

My hand swept over the crowd of demons. "From them!"

Pepper turned to me with bright eyes. "My dear little teacup, why do I need to escape from my enclave?" Her smirk curled with smug amusement setting off my short fuse.

"You did the same for me."

From across the room Eli groaned with exasperation, his eyes pointed to the ceiling.

She ignored him. "I've always allowed my progeny to leave this life behind..." Pepper looked at my neck and wrinkled her nose. "But I've never had any come back to 'save me.'"

"She's loyal to you." Eli deigned to speak. "I told you, we can have more than one grown blood doll."

Mother narrowed her eyes and turned to Eli. "No."

"The hell, I'm not staying here!" I barked.

Pepper smiled at me. "There's my bitter leaf. I suppose your stubbornness will lead to your death. Very well, your enclave against mine."

"What?" I was stunned. "What do you mean?"

"I suppose you only have your pitiful humans." She looked down at Thomas a moment, then glided to the bar. Her steps pitter-pattered as she passed the kneeling Dracule. Each vampire dipped their head in reverence as she passed. I watched her go, too stunned to stop her, too stunned to move or even breathe.

She faced us when she stood by Eli's side and petted the top of his head. "I've always allowed my progeny one chance to live life, my daughter. One chance." She cast her eyes down at Eli, the eldest of the Florentine brothers.

"Pepper," Eli begged. "Let's talk about this. She could be useful in your experiments."

She stopped and thought, then shook her head. "Ever the romantic," she sighed, then her voice hardened. "Kill her, my dark gems, and I'll reward you. Oh, and Thomas, if you're the one to destroy her, I'll forget about your failure." She looked down to Eli. "See, my sweet? I can be lenient."

Kill me? My mind went numb. This was not how this was supposed to go. I didn't want to kill anyone. Not even those that had literally drained my youth. I just wanted my mom and me to get out of here alive.

Thomas struggled. His lips moved but no words came out. Remaining crouched in a fighting stance, his head stayed immobile while his eyes whipped from right to left. A chill spread across the room. Five from the crowd crept closer. Shadows in the background stepped forward and coalesced into more enemies, more people, it seemed, than the room could hold. A hiss warned me from behind. The door was now blocked by a raven-haired Dracule.

"Mother?" I implored her to turn around. To look. This wasn't right. She was brainwashed. Had to be. There was no other reason why my mother would want me dead.

She ignored me and went to the stairs.

I stood there, unable to move. Nothing registered. A wave of confusion kept me at a standstill while something inside me screamed for me to move.

She veered left and climbed the steps until she was out of sight without a second glance.

CHAPTER 14

"WHAT HAVE YOU DONE to my mother?" My eyes flew to Eli.

The slick bartender paid no attention to me and, with steel in his glare and sarcasm in his voice, said to Thomas, "Well done, brother. You were supposed to keep her away from the enclave, and now look what you've done."

I looked at the vampire I'd started to trust with a heart full of malice. His eyes expressed sorrow, but I wasn't buying his silent plea.

Tears brimmed my eyes. I'd started to like Thomas, but he was the enemy. "You're one of them, right?"

Thomas's body shook with effort, but he remained kneeling.

"Answer me, dammit!"

Eli's voice whispered in my ear so close I could feel his breath. "Food doesn't talk."

I swung around, throwing my fist at Eli in reflex, but all I caught was air.

Eli stood by the bar as if he hadn't moved.

"Quinn." Eli motioned to one of the shadows in the crowd. "Come here."

The darkness parted, and a man in a hoodie stepped from the shadows. He had the same build and the same jacket as when I saw him on Eustachys's recording. My eyes went wide and my breath hitched. Military Jacket guy stood beside Eli. As Quinn had his hands in his sweater pockets and his hood over his face, I couldn't discern what he looked like, but his build was the same as on camera. From what I could tell, his physique resembled a quarterback, sleek but strong.

The head bloodsucker hovered closer to Quinn. Eli reminded me of a comic book badie's sidekick, slithering around his prey. Eli set the tips of his fingers on Military Jacket guy's shoulders as if Quinn's clothes would burn Eli, and said, "Tell me, Quinn, how do you think our Liebling's daughter found us? Hmmm?"

Petting Quinn's head like he would a dog's, Eli skulked like a cheap mob boss in his wetted-down blond hair. Quinn didn't answer.

The head vampire gripped the top of Quinn's hood and pulled Military Jacket guy's head back and grabbed his throat. "She recognized you. Could it be you've been leaving crumbs for this little rat to find us?"

Quinn gripped Eli's arm like a lifeline but otherwise said nothing.

"Bah!" Eli tossed his captive like a freshly used tissue. Quinn fell into the table and chairs, taking the set down with him.

"Prove yourself, Quinn," Eli said in disgust. "Do as our Liebling says."

He was going to kill me. My mother had asked him to. It was the most unreal feeling.

Quinn lifted his head as he stood up, and I could see one piercing yellow eye cut through to my soul.

"Isn't she like her?" Quinn asked.

"Don't make the same mistake as my brother over there." Eli thinned his lips and waved a hand at Thomas. "You already have a queen, and she has given you an order."

Their attention went to Thomas, who shook, his face in a mask of fury. Spurts of air hissed through his teeth, but he still didn't speak.

Maybe he couldn't because my mother told him not to?

"Thomas," I whispered. "Get up."

He tried. His body shook with violent tremors. Droplets of sweat cascade from his temple. Then, his body relaxed but his eyes cast toward me in a defiant glare. His mouth bobbed like he wanted to speak.

Eli laughed. "Miles didn't so much as give you a drop of blood. Poor Thomas. This is where all your idealism has wrought. It must gall you to know that redemption is in your grasp, and it goes against your precious morals."

Thomas snarled but otherwise didn't move.

"Hey!" I stomped a foot at Eli. His taunts lit a fuse in my heart. "He's not the monster here. What have you done to my mother?"

"Quinn." Eli soured. "Or you, Thomas. First one to kill her will be forgiven. Last chance."

Well, crap. Death was a real possibility. It dawned on me that I might not get out of this one by body bag. I'd always avoided tight squeezes by being dead, but I might not come back this time.

Quinn turned, hesitating, but I could see the one yellow eye calculating a decision.

Thomas struggled for a little bit, then closed his eyes, and bowed his head. "Fine. Have it your way."

Wait, wait, wait. "Thomas?"

His expression turned from frustrated to resigned. He rose to his full height in a single, smooth movement. "Sorry, Miles."

"Be grateful, Miles," Eli said. "Thomas has been protecting you for—how long?—a decade. You should give up your life in return."

"You mean spying on me." I glared at my Dracule neighbor. "At the coffee shop, you acted oh so gallant."

"I was teaching you a lesson," Thomas said, his voice cold, his expression shuttered. "One you still haven't learned."

He was certainly going to demonstrate whatever his point was today.

Thomas stepped toward me and Eli blocked him. The intensity Thomas aimed at his brother framed the light, highlighting his piercing blue eyes. Déjà vu. The glint in those eyes took me back to when I was twelve. The last thing I saw before I escaped were those pair of glacial blue daggers that said—never come back.

Thomas turned his eyes on me and pushed his brother aside, but not before Eli gripped his shoulder and said, "I'm trusting you. Do the smart thing."

My vampire neighbor pointedly looked at Eli's hand. "Eli, sometimes, I desperately hate you."

A rush of air, a familiar sting at my neck, a body pressed up against me, and the sensation of falling came all at once. Time stood still. I had a moment wondering if maybe Professor Nightshade might find my remains and teach the class over my body. I hadn't had time to finish my homework for his class. Lightning killing those people only had one explanation that made sense to me. Paranormal powers. Would Warren be happy I was gone? Would anyone miss me?

"Traitor!" Eli screeched, and time sped up.

"What did I tell you?" Thomas angrily whispered in my ear. "Your back to the enemy!"

Then he was gone.

What just happened?

Taking stock, I was lying on the sticky bar floor. My hand flew to my neck, and I pulled back blood. Thomas had bitten me. He'd been hell-bent on getting my permission before. Why bleed me without consent now? He'd played high-and-mighty at the coffee shop. That's right. He'd allowed me the corner but told me why we should trade seats. He wanted my back to the enemy so he could protect me. Our conversation on the way here also had a sense of timing as well. Like he knew we were coming here.

A dervish of snarling, fighting, and breaking wood pulled me back into my right mind. As I lay on the pasty surface, I had a good look at the room.

Billows of smoke settled on the ground. I knew that cloud of death and had experienced it firsthand. Warren. The devil of ash and fire was here. I never thought I'd be so happy to see smoke.

I sat up and a chair flew over my head.

What the hell was going on? Was Thomas trying to save me or not?

Growling sent the tiny hairs on my neck vibrating. Through the haze, I got a look at a Dracule prowling to me on all fours. Gray face, severe cheekbones, extended canines, and while the face was human, something was not human about it.

I'd already been bitten once, and this time I was not going down without a fight. I reached in my pocket and pulled out the short cylinder I was feeling for.

Frick! The Dracule leaped for me. I snapped the laser pointer on and aimed, hitting the it in the eye. It screeched and landed on the floor before me. I scrambled away before it could recover. Adrenaline surged through me like a lightning bolt. My heart raced as I pushed myself against the wood seating well of the bar. The creature writhed, clutching its face with a long-fingered hand, its growls morphing into a menacing whine that sent chills down my spine.

I couldn't hesitate. I had a moment to gather myself. Fear surged back, but determination followed quickly on its heels. I scrutinized my surroundings because a laser pointer alone would not hold back a thirsty Dracule. The bar was littered with debris and shadowed by the soft lighting of the bar, but I spotted a broken bottle on the floor. The long neck of the glass had some jagged edges.

With the monster momentarily incapacitated, I slid across the grimy tile. I couldn't let the monster get its bearings. I aimed the laser pointer at the creature again, but I'd caught it by surprise before. It would be ready for me the next time it leaped. The eerie glow cut through the darkness, illuminating its twisted features as it began to rise.

"Stay down!" I shouted, though I didn't expect it to listen.

The Dracule was closing in, raw fury etched onto its ugly face.

Not wasting the advantage, I scrambled to my feet, adrenaline coursing through my veins as I snatched the nearby broken bottle and readied myself. The creature took a step back, the damage done to its eye turning it momentarily half blind and more vicious.

With a speed that belied its sickly frame, it charged again, the wild fury replaced by primal desperation.

"Not today!" I yelled back, feeling a surge of empowerment. With weak knees and shaky hands, I lunged forward, thrusting the glass shard toward the soft flesh under its jaw.

The impact was jarring. Warmth pulsed beneath my fingers as I drove it in, twisting with every ounce of force I had left. The creature gasped, a wet, gurgling sound, as its body went rigid for a moment before it rolled it's good eye at me... and laughed.

Breathless and shaking, I staggered back, trying to process what happened. The fight wasn't over. The Dracule stayed on its feet, gurgling in mirth.

Gripping the laser pointer tightly, I readied for another attack.

Its smile grew cruel and wide.

This time, I didn't think it would give me time to react.

Thick smoke billowed behind it, hot and fast like an erupting volcano. Then the Dracule was enveloped into the smoke, and my attacker disappeared as the cloud pulled away from me. An inhuman screech, a definitive crunch, a plop, then nothing. Warren. My very own Balrog saved me.

This was my chance to once more try to get my mother and get the heck out. All reason about her had left me.

Perhaps her command to kill me was a ruse to give me a chance to escape?

I rose, searched my jeans pocket for a scarf, and tied it around my neck. Not twenty-four hours ago, I'd healed enough to not have to wear one. Such was my luck.

Warren's thick cloud of a body expanded across the room. His smoke floated waist high but thinned out where a blur of motion in a suit and tie held off five Dracules. Thomas.

As Thomas had been dispatched by Warren so easily, I hadn't known Thomas could fight, but he was a wild cat defending himself. Though he had skill, five on one wasn't good odds. But the stairway was now unguarded. I ran for the place I'd seen my mother last and stopped in the alcove. It led to a way up and a way down.

The black hole going down squeezed the air out of my lungs. Mother went up. I didn't have to go down that panic-inducing channel of claustrophobia. Voices hissed in the darkness, calling my name. I froze. Like a little girl. Hell, at that moment, I was a terrified child staring down the halls waiting to be taken to that room of needles.

"Miles!" Thomas yelled.

I snapped out of my fear and turned around... just in time for a Dracule to slam into me.

Down we went. My laser pointer jumped out of my hand during contact. I tucked my head to keep my noggin from bouncing on the concrete. Half a second felt like a day. The Dracule-projectile turned around mid-flight like a cat. It was Quinn—Military Jacket guy. This close, I got a good look at him.

He wasn't like the other Dracules. It was like his transformation—or whatever it was that changed people into vampires—had gone wrong. He didn't look fully human. Yellow eyes, sickly skin, exaggerated features were enough to make him look "off" enough that people would at least look at him strangely. In my world, he wouldn't pass as human. Yet he did the most human act of anyone. Quinn wrapped his arms around my neck and spine as if to protect me.

My shoulders hit the stairs first, cushioned by Quinn's arm. The concrete was jarring after so much time in the air. If Quinn hadn't had a limb around me, my neck would have taken the brunt.

We tumbled head over heels. No matter how much Quinn tried to protect me, he couldn't save all of me. We tumbled, and the right cheek of my ass hit square on flat wood. My knee crashed against the corner of a stair. That would leave a mark. Then my foot went between the banister iron bars and yanked. Ouch! My ankle. It might not be broken, but I wasn't going to run in the foreseeable future even if I got out of this debacle.

The rest of the way down, I screamed. My everything throbbed, especially my foot, even before we stopped falling. It took an eternity to stop bouncing off the steps until we landed in a heap.

Fog dissipated the light from upstairs leaving the downstairs room in a gray haze. Quinn's not so squishy body lay motionless. I dare not move, not knowing if Quinn was friend or foe, whether the reason he saved me was to have me himself or for a more altruistic reason.

"Ma'am?" Quinn whispered.

Seriously? Ma'am? "Do I look that old to you?"

A pause, then he said, "Don't move."

All the blood rushed to my throbbing ankle, reminding me it was hurt. I whimpered out a curse. "Not sure I can."

Upstairs, the scuffle of feet and an occasional crash were the only indication a fight ensued. No roars of thunder or loud booms signaled a rumble. Michael Bay would be thoroughly disappointed. It made sense for two reasons. Smart predators don't announce their attacks, and if you want to live unnoticed, as all Dracules do, you don't make a lot of noise.

Quinn stiffened which set me on alert right before I heard a hissing sound.

I jerked against Quinn's arm around me to my ankle's angry protest.

"The ferals are down here." Quinn near squeezed my insides out as I squirmed in his hold.

"What does that mean?" I'd heard that term before from Diego, but still didn't know what it meant. My eyes started adjusting to the lack of light, and within the shadows, I could make out the shape of a man.

From his pallor, I guessed he didn't see the light of day much. His eyes were too large in his skeletal head. Leathery skin stretched over his face but didn't pad the bone underneath. He wore a poncho type robe fit for a banshee. Thin arms and legs stuck out from under the rags, and his hands were clawlike with very little meat on his palms.

The gaunt man blinked at me. His mouth open and salivating.

Quinn moved his head in an awkward position to see the pale-faced person. "Casper."

Casper gave no response. He stood there staring at me.

"Casper," Quinn said, raising his voice.

But the man in rags remained unresponsive.

"Ma'am?" Quinn looked to me. "I'm going to release you, but don't try to move, okay?"

"My ankle," I whispered.

"I know. Stay calm." He pinned me with his catlike eyes.

"Don't tell anyone to stay calm. That's insulting."

Quinn blinked. "Sorry, ma'am."

Ugh. Only I would be thinking of propriety at this moment.

From the darkness, I heard the scuffle of bare feet on concrete. My gut clenched. I knew that sound well from when I didn't own shoes and was used for food. My eyes adjusted to the lack of lighting, and I saw people surrounding us, keeping to the shadows. Pale faces, gaunt bodies, their clothes dirty and tattered. Some of them clung to each other. Others stood crouched as if ready to spring into action. Their eyes tired and desperate.

"Is this what you meant"—anger crept into my voice—"by ferals?"

They were people. Haggard, dirty, starving victims of Dracules.

"Ma'am..." Quinn gripped my arm.

Casper stepped forward. "She's like her."

"Wait, my friend." Quinn slowly got to his feet, raising his hands out like he was dealing with raptors. "We don't know this woman."

"Anyone is better than her." Casper swallowed, and his eyes fixated on my throat. He was acting like a Dracule smelling the blood from my puncture wound.

"Miles is her daughter."

Casper went still. I hadn't noticed his slow pace, but he'd been inching toward me.

"No." Casper moved oh so slow again. "This one sees us."

"All the better to manipulate us," Quinn said.

Casper brought his full attention to Quinn. "And how is it you are so strong to resist the call of this one's blood? Why are you the one that can walk free?"

"I'm not under her influence." Quinn remained eerily still. "I'm their plaything. If I break, then the rest of you don't stand a chance."

"It's already too late for us." Casper's sharp canines peeked out and pinched his bottom lip. The telltale teeth weren't long like Thomas's or Warren's, but enough to notice.

Well, craptastic.

I took another look at the huddled circle of people. Worn clothing, haggard faces, pale skin, desperation in their eyes. I got a better look at the ones creeping closer. A few kept swallowing—like they hadn't had a meal in a good long while, and I was on the menu. Quinn called them ferals, and I'd thought that's what he called food. But I was wrong. I didn't know what they were, but they weren't wholly human.

Quinn and Casper stared at each other. Their distraction gave Warren, in his silent fog form, a chance to float down with a vengeance. Smoke permeated the room and went into mouths, noses, and ears. Yet no one coughed. I don't think they even noticed. Was I the only one that could see him? See his plan? A sick feeling churned in my stomach.

Warren's familiar whiskey-and-spice voice huffed from behind my ear. "You are becoming much more trouble than you're worth, Miles."

I backed into a solid form. I'd felt that chest under my hands in dreams. I dared not look to see if it was the human form or the muzzle and teeth. He was my only option. If I wanted to leave this place alive, I needed him right now.

"Warren, don't." Please don't, I tried to force the thought into his head. "I haven't been attacked. Quinn saved me."

"Thomas is one too many to commune with." Warren's whisper rasped in my ear.

What the hell? Commune?

Warren's muzzle sidled up next to me as he growled at a woman whose tattered jeans and T-shirt had seen better days.

"Please." She reached out to me and whispered, "I don't want to belong to her."

I made sure to keep my voice low. "Who is her?"

"The other one." She beckoned me with a hand, and eager eyes.

"You mean Pepper?" I asked.

"Shhh..." She pulled back and stared at the door above as if death itself would come for her.

"Why don't we ask the lady?" Casper spoke with effort—like smoke was in his throat. Though he didn't notice Warren's intrusion otherwise. It was as if none of them saw him.

Quinn and Casper turned their questing eyes to me.

"Ask me what?" I stepped back and smoke enfolded me like a blanket. Warren's presence was comforting and terrifying because he would keep me safe but watching him dispatch another's life wasn't something I wanted to witness.

"Mistress," Casper began. "We will serve you. You'll be ours..."

The Balrog I knew, and sometimes loathed, rushed forward with a body of billow and smoke, his muzzle and teeth bared.

"No," Warren growled.

Casper's already wide eyes grew larger. Screams of terror cried from the darkness. Quinn stepped back, masking his face with his hoodie. That confirmed it. They hadn't seen him. It must have seemed like a demon appeared out of thin air.

Warren's muzzle turned to me. "This is all I can give you, Miles. One warning. I will not be part of your enclave of Dracules."

Was there anything I could do? My ankle wouldn't let me put pressure on it. Warren was going to murder these people. I didn't want to go back to where I had come from, but I didn't want to kill anyone to get what I wanted.

"I just want to get my mother and get out of here."

Hope died in Casper's eyes. Quinn gave a heavy sigh. I hated delivering bad news. It was the truth. If they saw me as a savior, well, I wasn't it.

A shadow from the doorway above spilled across the stairs. I looked to see the slight frame and long hair of Pepper, my mother. She examined a laser pointer between her thin fingers and mused, "Like mother, like daughter."

At Pepper's appearance, Casper, Quinn, and the others shrank away to the walls. They were terrified of her, doing everything they could to become small, avoiding notice.

"So," she said, "it's true. You influence the angel of death."

Warren snarled. "I do not presume to take Azrael's place."

Cold blue eyes saw me through the darkness. She looked straight at me.

"Mom, what have they done to you?"

Pepper sniffed. "Are you sure you're my progeny? I've never had one so daft."

What do I say to that? "Maybe I'm completely mental. Either way, you're coming with me."

All of this was enough. I'd come so far to find her—hurt ankle and all, I made a hobble for it and limped to my mother. I planned to grab her and get out of this place. Get her therapy. She had to have been brainwashed. Hell, we both needed it.

A growl echoed in the basement. Heavy footsteps followed behind me, like a crowd of people running. My single focus was on getting up the stairs.

"Ma'am!" Quinn grabbed me and pulled me to him before I could grab the banister.

My whole leg was on fire.

Screams of horror. Wet splats. Flesh being rendered. I didn't dare look behind me.

Quinn let me go as he cried, "Casper!"

The Dracule dropped to his knees next to a flesh heap on the ground. There, in the middle of the floor, for all to see, was Casper, bloodied and unmoving.

Warren floated his bloodied muzzle and teeth beside me, blocking the stairs, preventing me from reaching my mother.

Pepper laughed. "Oh, you poor thing. You have no control over him, do you?"

Warren's muzzle slowly turned to her and growled low like a dog ready to strike.

My mother smiled with a Cheshire grin and wagged her finger. "Be wary, Guardian of Death. That is if you want to keep her to yourself."

The people surrounding us changed from cowering in fear to a swaying mindlessness. Even the mother holding her daughter stood. Any who were cowered straightened. The docile people now posed in an aggressive stance. Two dozen eyes looked at me like prey. These ferals, as Quinn called them, grew a dangerous aura about them.

All but Quinn himself had changed. He remained on the floor scooping the remains of Casper into his arms. After the fact, I knew the stupidity of what I'd done. Quinn wanted me motionless so I wouldn't attract attention. When I made a sudden movement as if I were escaping, Casper, like any Dracule, had gone after me. Warren intercepted Casper, while Quinn tried to block his friend from attacking me. That was two, possibly three, times Quinn had tried to protect me.

I was too afraid of what might happen if I raised my voice above a whisper. "Warren?"

His smoke filled their lungs, and it terrified me of what he was capable of.

"I'll be leaving now." Mother turned with a smile on her face, not seeing the shadow behind her.

Thomas, his crystal-blue eyes glimmering under the stark contrast of blood over his face, blocked my mother's path. "No. You won't."

He looked larger, wider, standing taller than ever. It took me a beat to figure out he'd been hunched over, diminishing himself to fit into the human world.

"Eli!" Mother tried looking past my neighbor, but I doubt she could see through Thomas's all-consuming aura blocking the way.

Thomas was not as tall as Warren—whose only rivals in height were basketball players—but the second-in-command of the Florentine Dracules could make himself look smaller than he actually was.

"Eli isn't coming." He sneered at her.

Mother turned and bore her wrath down on me. "Tell him—"

Thomas grabbed her by the throat and pinned her to the wall. The laser pointer she held clattered to the floor. With vicious scorn and fury in his eyes, he brought his lips close to smearing blood over her silken hair. "You can no longer tell me what to do by proxy or otherwise."

"How dare you touch me!" Pepper's eyes alighted with rage.

All hell broke loose. The ferals lunged for me. Wet explosions, reminiscent of slicing into a ripe watermelon, splattered flesh and brain matter across the walls. Headless bodies flopped to the concrete. I couldn't make out if Quinn was among those destroyed, but my heart went out to all of them anyway.

"Why?" I looked to Warren. My foot throbbed to the beat of my heart. Still, the hurt in my chest overshadowed my physical pain.

The muzzle permeating out of ash tilted down. "I would not let them harm you, nor feed from you."

"Are you going to kill Thomas, too?" Technically he did feed from me, but I think I understood why. My blood gave the Dracule the power he needed.

Warren didn't answer.

I moved through the smoke to the stairs' handrails. Thomas held Pepper by the throat, with a murderous glare, while my mother held a condescending smirk on her face, like she was the one with the upper hand.

"Thomas, please don't kill her." I used the strength in my arms to hop up the steps.

My mother laughed, and Thomas grimaced in disgust. Her mirth was cut short when he tightened his grip around her throat, and she started coughing.

Warren's muzzle floated beside me. "Remember, your words are power. Control what you say."

"Which is why I said please," I quipped back. "Even knowing he's a Dracule."

Smoke billowed around me. A part of me thought he was trying to help me up the steps even knowing I didn't want his touch.

Pain fogged my reasoning. Warren's form soared up the stairs with me to the top, and those sharp teeth came very close to Mother's face. "Her blood does not constrain me. Watch yourself."

Mother shifted her head to him and smiled. "Your mother was just here, looking for you."

The monster of ash and teeth sneered, and a fierce swirling of emotion churned around in my heart. She was goading him. I did everything I'd learned to keep calm over the years so my emotions wouldn't stir in the mix of Warren's feelings. I feared he would take the bait and kill her.

By some miracle, I rushed to my mother, got in between her, and Warren, taking the brunt of his loud, angry roar.

Spittle flew in my face and hair. In part, it was a relief. I thought for sure he'd rip her apart.

"I won't let you kill her." I wiped my face with a hand, using the other arm to block him in case he wanted to chomp down on her head.

"She's not worthy to live." His jaws and teeth snapped.

"Don't you believe in redemption?"

Warren pulled back as if I'd slapped him. Stillness, as if I were the only person breathing, brought my attention to my mother clawing at Thomas.

"Let her go," I growled at him.

Thomas sneered and started shaking. Exactly like when Pepper told him to kill me. His eyes bore pure hate onto me, and it left me breathless.

Warren growled low and long in warning at Thomas.

I didn't quite understand, but I knew Thomas was fighting me. Rather, to be precise, he was fighting my words.

"Please." It was difficult to look into his expression of pure malice. "Let her breathe."

One heartbeat later, Pepper gasped in a breath. I let out my own sigh of relief. Thomas too, breathed hard, pointedly looking at me with barely contained anger.

"Thank you, Thomas," I said, and his fierce gaze softened.

We were at a stalemate. Mom didn't want to die. I didn't want her killed. Warren and Thomas would have murdered her themselves if I'd had a weaker resolve.

Bodies littered the ground downstairs, and the smell of flesh and blood overwhelmed me. My ankle was throbbing—but it could have felt a lot worse. Thick smoke gathered around my hurt leg, and somehow, I believed Warren had something to do with controlling the pain to a manageable level. My confusion reigned overall.

There were pieces I thought I understood, but nothing connected.

"Let's bring this down a notch." Maybe I could talk my way through this.

"She's evil, Miles." Thomas turned to Pepper. "She pitted me against my whole family."

Mother's voice came out hoarse. "And why did I do that, Thomas? Who betrayed us first?"

"You're sick! An illness! We were better without you! The world is better without you!"

Before he could block her air again, I went to soothe him, stepping forward extending my hand. "Whoa, whoa, Thomas."

With his free arm, he slapped my hand back, the pain sharp, agony streaked down to my ankle, sending me reeling to the basement. Warren solidified into his human self and blocked me from having a second tumble down the stairs.

"Watch yourself," Warren growled. Even with this messed up situation, wearing his sexy suit and tie, Warren's voice tingled down my spine. I thought he'd been talking to me, but when I looked at him to quip back, I wasn't the one he was glaring at.

Pepper sniffed. "You need to bring these two in hand, daughter o' mine. Less they end you."

"They aren't mine to control."

"Ah, but they are. Otherwise they—" She coughed.

Thomas put the squeeze on her voice box. At the same time, a ping emanated from Warren's coat pocket.

"Excuse me." Warren dug into his pocket. "Kill her or don't, Thomas, but don't let her go." He turned and scanned his phone, going up the stairs.

"Wait..." Call me needy, but at that moment he was my security blanket. The one that could stop Thomas if things went south. However, at this moment, Thomas and he were aligned in thought.

Warren turned, and in an uncharacteristic move, he set light fingertips to my cheek. "Miles, you are better off without me. I'm only instigating Thomas to kill her. It's what I would do. But I know how much she means to you. So, I'm bringing in a partisan party to secure her. She won't be harmed if you can convince Thomas not to take her life."

I blinked. "Who are you, and where's Warren?"

He chuffed. "I've been emotional as of late. I don't think many like to be a slave to the whims of another." Warren gave a nod to Thomas. "He does bring a certain balance to the fold. Use reason, and he will follow your lead."

Another piece of the puzzle clicked. "Warren, nothing I say to you or Thomas is a command. I'm asking, never expecting for obedience."

Warren stared at me as if sussing out my words. He glanced at Pepper, then at me again, and his whole demeanor changed. The suspicion I'd seen in his eyes vanished. His dour expression unmasked to a vulnerability I'd not seen in him since he held my hand when he thought I was dead.

"I can feel you speak truth." His shoulders dropped half a centimeter, and his stiff attitude relaxed.

"Feel me?"

One side of his lips quirked. "Everything. I feel everything. When you're sad, happy, horny, hurting"—he glanced at my ankle—"I'll say it as many times as you need for it to sink in. I can feel you. And now, so can Thomas."

Oh God. Now Thomas had a pipeline to my emotions. Fantastic.

I turned my head to Thomas. Could he not snap my mother's neck because he felt my love for her? Was he fighting it? A bond with blood dolls seemed more than with Normans.

Despite his newfound trust, Warren was holding back, but if my thoughts were right, I didn't blame him.

"Oh!" I turned back to Warren. "Does my blood also have this weird control over him?"

He smirked and used one of my own lines against me. "I don't know how the science works. I just know it does."

So many questions. How long does the bond last? Wasn't Thomas free after he bit me? My heart sank. He didn't say it, but he was a slave—to me of all people. I didn't want that for anyone.

Warren lifted his chin. "He must have had her blood a long time ago and not have taken any blood since. Until you." Warren squinted his eyes and sighed. "I suppose I know what it's like."

"Thank you. No one's ever explained the other side to me." All I knew about blood dolls was from experience. I knew what it was like to give but not receive.

"Don't get used to it." Warren turned and tromped up the stairs.

Before, I might have thought his words and actions rude. Now, I understood them as his defiance against the chains my blood wrapped around his will.

When I looked back, my mother couldn't breathe again. I brought up all my love for her and tried a different approach. "Thomas?"

His face twisted in a grimace of pain, and tears streamed from his eyes. "Don't ask me to spare her."

"You said she pitted you against your family, yet you want to do the same to me."

He inhaled sharply. His vulnerable eyes cast a question. "Am I your family?"

Had I meant it that way? A breath. A moment. A thought later. "You know, it'd be nice to have an older brother."

Thomas smiled, but Pepper's face turned from pink to red.

"Hand her over, Florentine." A shadow glided up to the alcove, and a familiar simp in glasses filled the doorway. "She's not going free."

"Diego." Thomas sneered. "Did you come running to your master's call."

"Of course I did." Diego pulled out a fluffy set of handcuffs from his coat pocket and scoffed. "Oops. Wrong ones." He put them away and pulled out real metal handcuffs. "Here we are."

"I don't know if I trust you to take this seriously." Thomas eased off his hold on Pepper's neck at least for her to breathe.

"I'm not the one whose loyalty can be swayed by blood." Diego swung the handcuffs around on his finger. "One trip with your teeth exposed, and your allegiance goes out the window."

Oh, if looks could kill, Diego would be smoldering ash.

"That's between me and Miles," Thomas said.

"And since she's Warren's too, that would include me."

Thomas lowered his head and swore.

Diego snapped a cuff around Pepper's wrist. "Well, at this rate, if I don't take her, she'll get brain damage."

"Good." Thomas sulked.

"No, not good." I clenched my hands.

Least he took my anger as permission for killing my mom, I breathed. Crap on toast, I'd have to wonder if he was reacting to me or to his own desires. It was enough to give me a headache.

Thomas smirked, and I could see the calculations behind his eyes. The term "two can play at this game" came to mind.

"Don't manipulate my feelings," he said. and handed Pepper over to Diego.

Warren's aide snapped the other cuff around her free wrist.

Throughout the revelations unfolding, Pepper absorbed my drama with cool eyes and a tight lip. Was my life parallel to hers? Or was this entertainment?

"Seems as though you are second with this family too, Thomas," my mother rasped.

"Uh-uh." I ticked my finger back and forth at her. "You don't get to diminish my friends."

"See." Thomas lifted his head and grinned. "Things are grandly different from your brood."

Sometimes, I could tell Thomas was an old-world soul by his word choice.

Metal on metal clicked, as Diego tightened the handcuffs around Pepper's wrists. "I'll take her to a special place where people can't bite her."

"In the ground would be better," Thomas mumbled.

One day, I'd have to find out why he was so hell-bent on her death.

I heard a girl's piercing scream, and my stomach dropped. Warren had found someone upstairs, and by the sound of that shriek, I wasn't going to like this one bit.

CHAPTER 15

"SHIT." I HOBBLED UPSTAIRS.

A flash in a suit rushed past me. Thomas got to the top of the second-story stairs before I did.

"Ah." Thomas sighed. "Right."

What the heck! Were there more Dracules? More ferals?

I passed the landing where the ground floor bar was and climbed the stairs to the second floor. When I got to the top, I came flush to Warren's upright back. The stiffness in his demeanor returned. He had his phone in his hand and stared off into the room. Between Warren and Thomas, I couldn't see much beyond them.

Warren let out a huff. "Were you going to tell me they were here?"

Thomas tsked. "I'm trying to preserve them. Not wipe them off the face of the earth."

"Excuse me." I wiggled between the two men—er... monsters—or whatever they were. When I broke through, my heart sank.

Children. Seven of them. All younger than me. All of them bore a strong resemblance to Pepper. Blond hair, blue eyes, pale skin.

The open room had rows of small beds on one side and a chest of drawers on the other. Each child was frozen in place like prey caught between a predator and escape. One little boy held a small suitcase in place as if pulling it off the bed, but paused in the middle of the action, petrified. A little girl clasped at her pink dress, her wide eyes staring at Warren. One older girl, maybe twelve, held another boy in diapers in her arms. The rest were in similar frozen states of fleeing but stuck like deer in headlights.

My head swung to Warren. His face went from appalled to resigned in the span of seconds. I could see him hardening his heart as his expression turned cold.

"No!" I swung around blocking his path.

Thomas jerked his head to Warren. "They're children."

"Children that will grow up to be just like Pepper," Warren mumbled as if he were trying to convince himself.

Thomas stared, opened mouthed, eyes flashing with conflicting morals.

"No." I held my arms out. "That's final." He was not going to unalive children.

Warren looked at me confused for a moment. His wary eyes could suck all the hope out of a Lollapalooza concert. "This is what I do, Miles."

I kept my voice down so the kids wouldn't hear me. "How noble."

He rubbed his face looking more haggard after his large hand dropped to his side. "Protecting mankind is my mission. They have to go to—"

"I have to agree with Miles." Thomas stepped up next to me. "There's another way."

Warren sneered. "Of course, the Dracule would want a brood of blood dolls. You could do so much with them.

Sell them. Breed them. Feed off them. Build an army. Ruin man and take Earth for yourself."

I heard a sharp intake of air behind me, and I worried that the eldest had figured out what was going on.

"Or," I countered. "Give them safe harbor, let them get jobs, let them live their life free from continuous pain and puncture wounds."

"To proliferate." Warren jutted out his chin. "To become victims and allow more and more Dracule to infiltrate this reality."

"You just said you protect mankind. I doubt you'd let that happen."

Warren threw his hands up, his fingers like claws of frustration. "And how do you think I do that? Someone has to make hard choices."

"And refuse to give anyone a chance?"

He looked ready to kill the nine of us right then and there. "I gave you a chance, and I'm starting to regret it."

"Go ahead then!" I stepped up to Warren not feeling one bit of the bravado of my words. "Fix your mistake."

"You dare think I won't?" Warren growled.

"No, I know you would. So go ahead!" I was calling his bluff.

Warren snapped his head, looking past me, and roared, "Thomas!"

I spun around. Bless him, the Dracule held the window open for the eldest girl who had the little boy in her arms. The other children had gathered with them to exit stage left.

"Oh God, Thomas, we're on the second story."

"They'll live." His desperate eyes gave me a glance before helping the girl over and out.

I ran to the window and pushed half my body outside. The girl was already too far down. I wanted to scream. In a blink, Warren was there holding his hands out, ready to catch her and the babe she held.

Out of the frying pan and into the fire.

They landed in his arms, safe. To my surprise, Warren didn't shred them right then and there. He held the teenager, kneeling to her level and started talking to her.

I could think the worst of Warren, but I knew better. He was a big softy. Warren needed a reason to spare them. I turned to Thomas who now had one little boy and girl in his arms. He was already headed to the stairs with the rest of the children following.

"Thomas!"

The seemingly altruistic Dracule didn't hesitate and kept going. "I can't take the chance, Miles."

I hobbled to catch up as he grabbed a third little girl and a fourth hopped onto his back, clutching his neck. He tucked them in close, looked back at the little boy with the suitcase and up at me. Then he was gone.

"No!" I limped after him, but it was useless. The stairs were empty. My ankle was shot. I had no chance to catch up to him.

The little suitcase boy stood inside the empty room, trembling, tears in his eyes, holding his luggage, using it like any other kid would a blanket.

"Oh, no, no, no. No tears." I crouched down before him. "I'm not going to let anything bad happen to you."

"My sisters left without me." He swiped at his eyes. He was scared and no doubt felt abandoned.

"You're very brave for letting your sisters go first." I gave him a soft smile hoping it would ease his fear.

The boy looked down at his suitcase. "I have all their clothes."

His words were a missile to my heart. The consideration for his family, or the practicality, or the hope that they'd need something to wear was more than I could take. "We'll find them. I'm somewhat stubborn when it comes to searching for people."

His eyes lifted with a hopeful gaze, and a soft voice asked, "Are you Chamomile?"

I breathed in sharp. "I prefer Miles, but yes, I'm Chamomile." Had Mother been talking about me? "What's your name?"

"My name is Soil, but I prefer Clay."

A disgusted sigh escaped my lips. "They still use the way you taste to name us?"

The little boy nodded.

"Well, Clay—"

"Miles!" Warren's angry tone shouted from the street below.

Frustration had me poking my head out the window. "What?"

"Call him back." He looked as frustrated as I felt.

"Who?"

"Thomas!" He held the teenager by the arm. "He took the others."

"I tried!"

"Did you try calling him with your blood? He can't disobey a direct order from you."

I looked up and down the alleyway. "Watch what you say."

"Miles." Warren clenched his jaw. "Call him back."

"How?"

"Don't play coy with me." Warren could burn a hole in my head with his piercing stare.

Argh! I ducked back inside and messaged my temples.

The rolling of suitcase wheels and a small body stepped beside me. "Think of the person you want to contact and then feel what you want them to feel."

I knelt down beside Clay and gazed into his soulful, knowing eyes. "Is that how I can call Thomas back?" Which wasn't the question I wanted to ask. What I wanted to ask was, How do you know? It was obvious. They hadn't spared him. Just like those monsters hadn't spared me.

Clay nodded.

I closed my eyes and thought of Thomas. The suave Dracule—who liked to scare people, who had stalked me for almost a decade, who told me all the things I wanted to hear—had taken off with a few child blood dolls. What was he going to do with them? I'd thought we were on the same page. He talked a good game, but he'd shattered my trust. It was difficult to believe his intentions weren't nefarious.

"Thomas, you son of a..." I let my anger lose. "Get back here with those children."

Nothing. Not a blip.

Determination kicked against my heart. I called out to Thomas in my mind. Warren isn't going to hurt them. We can change his mind.

Still nothing.

I sighed, looked to Clay, and shook my head.

"Oh, well, sometimes they rebel." He gazed down with a stare that made me think he was a million miles away.

"Come on, kiddo, let's go downstairs before that Balrog eats half your family."

Clay put his hand in mine. "Okay, big sis." He pulled his little suitcase behind him.

I had to choke back my own tears. "Want help with your suitcase?"

"No." He gripped the handle tightly. "I can get this."

No need to destroy his pride by pushing my own desire to be useful. Taking away someone's agency was the worst thing to do in the name of helping them.

He awkwardly got his luggage down the stairs, while I bit my tongue and kept my hands to myself.

However, I couldn't refrain from asking questions. "How long have you been here?"

We got down the flight of stairs when he took my hand again. "We move a lot. But we've been here through the summer."

Sounded about right. Three or four months I was guessing.

I led us through the bar. Tables lay askew. Chairs lay everywhere but on their legs. Any liquor still in bottles was leaking onto the floor. The place looked like there'd been a brawl. I wish I didn't have to bring him this way, but unless we wanted to jump out a window, it was the only way out.

"Is it only the seven of you?"

Clay nodded, unfazed by the destruction. Just another Tuesday.

"How old are you?"

"Seven. I'm fourth oldest. I have a lot of re-spawn-see-bill-eh-ties."

It was all I had to stop from snorting out loud. The kid was the serious type. I doubt he'd appreciate me laughing at his—responsibilities.

When I'd barged in, looking for my mother and finding Eli, I hadn't seen a visible exit. I expected to find nothing but a brick wall, but the secret door remained open.

A gasp and a tiny hand tugged me to a stop. I expected a threat. Eli standing in our way. Some kind of cheap shot you'd find in a B thriller movie, but there was nothing.

"What's wrong?"

Clay stared at the door. "My sisters..."

"What's happening? Can you feel them?"

He looked up at me and whispered, "They don't have any clean underwear."

Did I get that right? "What?"

His little eyes dropped to his luggage. "Do you think that guy will get them new underwear?"

I was flabbergasted. He was worried about underpants? Not "will they be safe?" or "is my family going to get eaten?" or "will I see them again?" I supposed he was just like his big sister. Propriety over reality.

"Ummm... ahhh..." I stammered. Was this an existential crisis? "You know," I said. "Thomas seems fastidious enough to think about that, so maybe we can give him the benefit of the doubt."

Clay peered into my eyes and relaxed. "Okay."

I limp-walked to the door with—most likely—my sibling and out into the alleyway.

"Let me go!" A shout down the alley echoed off the brick buildings.

A familiar growly voice down the aisle answered, "I abhor liars."

"I'm not lying!"

I stiffly walked to Warren with Clay in hand when the little boy tore away from me and rushed down the alley. "Let her go!"

Warren turned with his phone to his ear, and the bewilderment across his face made me want to believe he could be a decent person. He tilted the phone back and answered the boy. "I will not."

The teenage girl spotted Little Suitcase boy. "Clay! Get out of here!"

She tugged and twisted, trying to get out of Warren's grip. She still held the other little girl in her other arm, but if it was free, I was sure she'd be hitting him too. "Get off me!"

Warren put his phone into a suit pocket. "Stop it."

Clay stood out of reach and started yelling, "Let my sisters go!"

I could see the moment Warren lost his patience. His left eye ticked, he grimaced, and I feared he'd end the teenager right then and there.

"No!" I jumped forward, putting myself in his arms and in between the girl.

"Miles, I've had it with all of you. I'm taking you all to the Brightwood Estate. I'm sure Diego will have a great time tormenting you all."

"Wait, you're what?"

"Freedom, Miles. Isn't that what you wanted most? Well, maybe Diego was right. Maybe you all should stay at the manor."

"You're not going to... you know..." I used the back of my finger to swipe under my chin.

"What?" Warren stepped back like I'd dealt him a physical blow the likes of Mike Tyson.

"Oh." Had I pegged him wrong all this time? "So, you're only taking them somewhere?" I didn't end my sentence with "you're not going to kill them?" For fear of frightening the children.

"They're still human." Warren stared at me in hurt disbelief.

"But the people downstairs..."

"They were ferals, yes, but..." His expression went from shocked to exasperated. Warren ticked off a finger. "They were suffering." He ticked off another finger. "They were going to attack you against their will." He ticked another finger. "And once a blood doll has you under their influence, you're done. They were Dracules. It's not a disease you can cure. They didn't want to attack you. They were forced. Do you want to relive your nightmare?"

I shivered at the recollection. "Weren't we talking about hard choices?"

"I was talking about them losing their freedom to go out into the world, yes. But they're children, Miles."

Gravel pelted Warren's suit, and we looked back to find Clay picking anything off the ground and throwing it at us. I suspected his target was the person holding his sisters.

"Clay, don't be mental." The teenager rolled her eyes. "You're hitting me too." She tugged without effect.

His antics put a smile on my face. Little Suitcase boy was relentless. He reminded me of myself.

"Let my sisters go!"

"Stop, you tweaker," the teenager said. "Are you not listening. He's not going to hurt us." She looked up at Warren. "Right, mister?"

"That depends..." Warren bared his teeth. "Are your slaves going to come after you?"

She sneered. "My what?"

"Warren," I said, cautioning him. I wasn't the only person Warren's personality grated against. "You pretty much offed everyone in the building, and if her life was anything like mine, she doesn't have any allies left if she ever had any."

"You had Thomas. Second to the Florentine Enclave."

"Thomas? Are you kidding me? Do you see him here now?" I swept a look around the alley with incredulous sarcasm.

"Fine." He relented. "I don't have time to deal with this. Diego isn't answering me."

"Heaven forbid your assistant not answer your every beck and call." Slave driver.

"You don't understand." Warren's body turned black like the night sky. "He always answers my call. There's something wrong."

Darkness expanded over me, crashing like a tidal wave, pulling everyone inside—into Warren.

"What the hell?" The teenager held on to her charge, who clung to her sister with wide eyes.

They were the first to disappear into Warren's black hole of a body.

"Warren! Where are you taking them?"

I heard a tiny battle cry. Suitcase and all, Clay charged with all the rage a seven-year-old could muster. Warren grabbed the boy and threw him into his black cloud ethereal body.

"You'll be safe, Miles." Warren floated to me.

"Wait, wait, wait! Warren, I don't want to go."

"No. I need you safe."

"Let's talk this out first." I held my hands up like a shield from the nothingness coming for me. "I'm safe by your side."

He wasn't listening. Something had him spooked, and no amount of reason could settle his nerves. Then his black-smoke body enveloped me.

Falling into this miasma was like walking into the portal from Warren's home to the Rusty Teapot. Only it was like the air was water. I could breathe, and I could move, and light emanated from somewhere, but night surrounded me and was as vast as the sky.

I couldn't see much beyond a few yards with nothing to see, except the two girls. The eldest wrapped her body around the youngest, each holding the other tight. I grabbed for the girls as a tiny seven-year-old's battle cry warped and echoed. It sounded as if he were a world away.

The teenager's wide eyes shone with unshed tears, clearly frightened.

Clay splashed into the mist, and as I swam for him, pulling the other two with me, I thought, Didn't he enter before I did?

As I reached for Clay, the Warren-sized hole we entered rippled a scene showing the alley behind him. I wrapped Clay and his sisters in a bear hug.

"Warren!" I yelled, spinning in this space, watching the opening close up. "Bastard!"

"Rose?" The little voice of a child echoed. "Clay?"

"Juice! Clay!" The teenager, even though she was right next to me, sounded so far away.

Somehow, they'd escaped my hold. I swung around, in this place where I couldn't touch anything, couldn't gain purchase, and floated in this nothingness.

I expected darkness, but the source of light floated closer. Bright as a star and as big as the sun, a ball of light hung in space, looming over me. Shielding my eyes with a hand, the hairs on my neck rose. Darkness turned to light, and I floated in white space. The initial fear faded. I felt safe and loved. Then I felt nothing at all.

CHAPTER 16

"HELLO AGAIN, CHILD." A soft melodic voice brought me to awareness.

"Michael?" I saw the kindly priest's face framed by windswept white hair. His crystal-blue eyes crinkled at the corners with laugh lines.

I sat on a familiar stone bench in a clearing of trees that stood as sentries, bringing a hush around the area. Michael knelt before me, holding my foot. Light glowed from his hands, and my ankle felt way better.

"Thank you."

He smiled wide. "Physical injury is not my forte, but this much I can handle."

"Why am I here?" And where was here?

"It's easier to talk to you this way."

"Last thing I remember..." Warren had pulled me... inside of him. Then all I knew was a single light in the darkness. "Did Warren put me in a holding bag?"

Michael scrunched his magnificent face in disbelief, then gave out a belly laugh. "I suppose you could interpret it that way."

Ugh. Great. "So, wait, am I dreaming again?"

His wide smile remained. "Isn't it all a dream?"

"More like a nightmare," I chided.

Michael gazed at me, and his scrutiny seemed more loving than critical. I felt safe and loved, and it gave me a chance to relax. I'd been rigid since I walked into the hellhole of Eli's bar. My body ached from carrying the weight of desperation to find my mother for so many years. Now that I had, the reunion I envisioned was nothing like reality.

"What have you learned thus far?" The corner of Michael's blue eyes crinkled.

The words came out without a thought. "That life is crappy?"

He studied me without judgement. "You don't wish to return?"

"I didn't say that."

His smile never faded. "Do you remember what I asked of you?"

"Something about getting to know the inheritor." Whoever that was.

"Oh, you know him, child. Let me show you."

An image appeared in my mind's eye. I saw the same scene of Warren's painting from his underground chapel. The last remaining demon stood in a corpse-riddled battlefield surrendering to a winged angel. Only, I saw the painting from the angel's viewpoint. The demon was the same one that had sucked me dry in the back of a limo.

"Warren? You're talking about Warren? He's the inheritor?"

Michael nodded.

"What's he going to inherit?"

"Everything." His smile grew wide and proud.

Okey-dokey. "I guess specific isn't your thing."

Michael laughed. "Since I've seen you last, you've gotten to know the inheritor a little more."

Heat rose in my cheeks. "A little."

To keep my sex dream with Warren to myself, I turned the conversation away from the memory. "Mother called him the guardian of death."

"She did." Michael wasn't fazed, like he'd heard it before.

"What did she mean by that?"

Michael tapped his lip with a finger. He thought for a moment and glanced at the trees. "What do you think, Chamomile? Protector of death isn't quite right. The real question is... What is death?"

His eyes cast a faraway gaze, his mind lost in his musing.

Fine by me. Anything to forget about my intimate dream with a demon. It was bad enough that it was a shared vision with said demon.

"So, Michael..." I hesitated because curiosity killed the cat, and I wondered if this question was worth one of my lives. "Are you, like, the Michael—as in heaven's Michael?"

He turned with a sly smile. "You've heard of me?"

How can someone be coy, smug, and gracious at the same time?

Michael's focus went past me. His expression drifted into less than a smile, he stood, and then turned to the trees. I followed suit and watched.

A looming figure in a fitted suit emerged from the oak sentries. Warren stepped onto the clearing with the air of a general facing off his enemy. He stopped at the edge where the circle of light and the shade of trees met and bowed at the waist, keeping his eyes on Michael.

"Michael," Warren said. "I see Grandfather is with you."

I looked around, but it was only Warren, me, and the famous angel.

Warren straightened and held out his hand to me. "Miles. Come."

I stepped closer to Michael. "So that you can shove me in your black hole again. No thanks."

Warren blinked. "Technically, you're still in my black hole, and I've come to get you out." He eyed Michael.

"Don't be angry with Him, child." Michael kept his smile, and his eyes softened toward Warren. "She called. We came."

"I still feel violated," Warren growled.

"Oh, child, when will you accept we are all one?"

An outpouring of light, love, and well-being spilled into the air. An all-consuming comfort flooded the space crowding out doubt and fear. I'd never felt safer, more cared for, or more at ease. There was nothing wrong in the world, nothing at all.

"Stop." Warren held a palm up. A mirror-black orb floated in front of his hand, absorbing the golden light spreading out over this tiny glen.

Holy... Warren staved off the power of God's number one angel like it was nothing of note. I did not want to admit that it was frightening and sexy in a twisted way.

Michael seemed genuinely sad, and spoke to Warren like a priest trying to save the damned. "I wish you would allow yourself to feel the love He has for you."

"I'm here for Miles. I'm not here to be influenced, and I don't want to argue with you or Grandfather." Warren's black orb dissipated, and he extended his hand to me once again. "Miles, I need your help. Will you come?"

"Why do you not call your goddess by her name?" Michael said.

Warren went deathly still. "My what?"

"Your goddess, or is the term 'soulmate'?" Michael smiled more in that knowing way to himself. "Such a silly saying."

"You're fu..." Warren stuttered. "You're confused. I took her essence in. It will dissipate. You're feeling the mingling of blood. She's not my mate."

"Every inheritor needs a counterpart." Michael remained steadfast.

Warren slashed his hand through the air, and the love weaving around us blew away like a rushing wind. "What scheme have you and Grandfather weaved into the fabric this time?"

The warmth of the glen returned but it was a softer tenderness than the intense euphoric joy.

It didn't faze Michael. "This has always been written, child."

"Written by His hand." Warren gritted his teeth. "I told Him I don't want it."

If they weren't talking about me being the inheritor's counterpart, goddess, mate, whatever, I'd bring out the popcorn and watch this family drama, but since this had something to do with me... "Hey, I don't want you either."

Warren seethed. "I'm tired of being manipulated. The three of you can—"

Michael rose to his full height and sniffed. He was not smiling. The air charged with electricity.

Warren let the rest of his words go unsaid. I wouldn't say he was cowed, but he certainly thought better of finishing his sentence, which made me evaluate Michael. Warren was powerful. He'd swiped away whatever Michael was doing with a wave. Yet the angel didn't even flinch. Warren was the type to let his fists—or teeth—do the talking. If the priest made him refrain, then that made Michael a whole new type of badass.

Michael winced as he looked at me and whispered, "Be not afraid, child."

Warren closed his eyes and breathed as if settling his nerves. Then he bowed at the waist once more. "My apologies. I will examine your words and learn why they invoke anger within me."

Warren glared at Michael, then turned and stalked off without another word.

The priest sighed. "Go after him, Chamomile." Michael gently pushed at my back.

"Why?" I was feeling salty. Warren put me in this place and now he was going to abandon me here? That and I was not sure I trusted myself being alone with him right now. My libido had a messed up sense of sexy.

"Only you can soothe his fears." Michael started disintegrating. Pieces of him floated up into the blue sky. Chunks of his body soared on the wind like butterflies as he gently smiled, his kind eyes gleamed with a knowing twinkle.

"Wait..." I grabbed for him, not wanting him to leave.

"We will meet again." The last fragments of Michael drifted away as our conversation echoed in my head.

I'd found out my mother had the potential to be a murdering kin killer and that Warren's claims that she might be doing something nefarious were not so far-fetched. I was in a black-hole world that was inside of another being. Newfound siblings were now lost or with

Thomas, someone I no longer trusted. I had problems, sure, but what did I know about Warren? He had come for me, and I needed to know why. It had nothing to do with having a powerful being at my beck and call when I felt like I was in trouble. After being alone for so long, it was natural to want someone to hold on to.

I ran to the oaks. "Warren? Wait!"

He stood as steadfast as the trees with his back turned to me. "I thought you wanted to go with Grandfather."

We stood there amongst the trees. His back to me. The sky turning from light to dark.

"Are you the devil?"

"What?" Warren turned around, his pale face and red-gold eyes—that could pass for brown at a distance—stared at me. His immaculate pinstripe suit made him look like a sexy Russian mobster. He looked alone. I knew how that felt.

"Is that what I am to you, a devil?" Warren's bewilderment was obvious. "Will I never have the chance to redeem myself in your eyes?"

I pointed to the trees behind us. "You stood your ground against an almighty angel."

"Archangel." His lips twisted, but I couldn't tell if he was angry or proud.

"You said you needed my help."

He huffed. I got the impression that his mind wandered in a sarcastically explicit direction. Something to the effect of, If I said I needed a BJ, would you still come running?

"Probably," I said—just to see if that was him in my head. "Cause, you know, Stockholm syndrome or whatever."

His expression turned serious. "Miles, I don't trust you."

"Well, I don't trust you either."

"But I need you," he said.

I felt the truth of that. I'd gone down roads where I had no one to trust, but I needed to move forward. "Trust implies that I can hurt you. I'm a gnat in your world. I don't see why you even need to trust me."

Warren massaged his forehead. "Did you not see how Pepper commanded those Dracules against their will?"

"I don't command you."

"Do you think I come to every maiden in distress?"

"I've never asked nor forced you to come to my aid."

"Thomas couldn't move against your mother until he drank from you. I've had an entire nine pints of your blood."

"Is that my fault?"

"Yes!" Warren held his fists against his sides.

I blinked. "You have the emotional intelligence of a teenager."

"I know!" He stood there, belligerent.

I waited for a heartbeat and then nearly keeled over laughing. "You're angry because you took something you needed and can't handle the consequences. That's what I'm getting."

The meaning to my words crashed into an understanding I'd been ignoring. An overwhelming pit of despair stopped my mirth cold. I'd hit the nail on the head. There was more in the truth of my flippant observation. He was afraid of what I might have him do, or what he would do for me. Behind that was loneliness that came from being different. I knew that sensation, too—feeling like you were the only one of your kind. That type of isolation dampened any joy, tore at hope, and put apathy into one's heart.

Seeds of trust were a place to start. They would either grow or wither. "My name is Chamomile Makayla Evans Eirian. Chamomile, thus, Miles. I was named after the taste of my blood."

His eyes widened, and a dam of emotions broke through me. Pity, sorrow, fear, relief, and something unnamed overwhelmed me.

He swept me in his arms, and his lips pressed against mine in a hungry, mindless abandon. I met it with my own urgency, as if our fiery connection could consume the very air. The world blurred into insignificance, leaving only the intoxicating heat that radiated between us—a potent mix of passion and danger.

His touch was electric, sending shivers down my spine as he cradled my face, his fingers trailing through my hair, like tendrils of smoke. I could feel his suit pressing against me. The warmth of his body enveloped me, drawing me closer. He possessed an otherworldly quality to him, a dark allure wrapped in shadows, The thrill of embracing a being so strong he could send light off to a distant corner of the universe sent my heart racing.

As the kiss deepened, I tasted the wildness of his essence—a mixture of night air and something ancient, something primal. His lips moved against mine with a fervor that left me breathless, awakening a hunger within me that I hadn't known existed. It was intoxicating and terrifying all at once.

I pulled back slightly, knowing full well that I was dancing on the precipice of something dangerous.

"Wait," I murmured, my voice above a whisper, but the fierce gleam in his eyes spoke of a determination I couldn't hope to resist.

In an instant, he lifted me, my legs wrapping instinctively around his waist as he pressed me against the bark of an oak. His body was a furnace, and with each passing moment, Warren's aura surged, filling the air with an intoxicating mix of power and desire.

"Do you fear me?" he growled, his voice a low rumble that vibrated through my chest.

I shook my head, emboldened by the wave of yearning that flooded me. "No," I breathed, feeling the truth of my statement. It wasn't him I was afraid of, but the strength of this connection. Warmth bloomed in my chest. His intensity softened, but power thrummed in my body.

"More," I said. Needing to face the tie of this blood bond.

My fingers dug into his shoulders, feeling the hard planes of his muscles beneath my touch. The shadows danced around us, flickering like fragmented memories illuminated by the ethereal light of the crescent moon above.

His hands roamed my body, exploring the curves and contours, elation sparking across my skin wherever he touched. Heat pooled in the pit of my stomach, creating a sweet ache. I had never felt so alive, so consumed by passion.

"Then let's embrace what we are," he purred, his breath a sultry caress against my ear. With that, he pressed his hips against mine, and I gasped at the sensation. The world around us faded—with only him against me and an ancient rhythm that pulsed in time with our heartbeats.

He captured my lips again, deeper this time, his tongue dancing as if to taste my very soul. I could feel the power thrumming in the air, swirling like the tendrils of darkness that cradled us. Whatever senses held me back now faded into the background, leaving only the raw, primal instinct of desire.

Each kiss set fire to my blood as he pulled me closer, the line between pleasure and pain blurring into something transcendent. My heart raced in response.

In that moment, I wasn't a girl standing on the edge of the abyss, I was an echo of our feral dance, caught in the whirlwind of his dark embrace. As his gaze locked onto mine, I realized there was no going back. We were destined to ignite.

"I'm going to fuck you mercilessly." His eyes burned with intent.

I gasped, a squeak of want escaped my lips.

"If you have a problem with that," Warren purred, "tell me now."

He waited, and I adored that he meant his words, that he would stop if I asked. Once I permitted the dam of desire to open, I would not be able to stop the flood. I would have to ride it out, and oh, what a journey it would be.

Warren nipped at my ear, sucking in my lobe and teasing the sensitive flesh.

"Yes." As soon as I said it, a spike of doubt shot from my heart to my stomach.

"Chamomile?" he whispered.

Crap. He'd felt that. "I'm okay. Yes, but no biting."

He smiled. "I won't bite you."

I nodded, feeling skin on skin. Through the haze of lust, I knew I forgot something and looked at his bare chest, then down at my own nakedness.

"How am I naked?"

Warren's chuckle rumbled, his voice rough like whiskey, and his breath smelled of burnt cedar. "We are still in my domain."

"Your domain?" The haze of lust coated my senses.

"Our shared dream was your domain. You are now in mine. I can do what I want here. Including dissolving your clothes."

"Oh." I smiled. "How convenient."

"Agreed." He pulled his hips back, revealed his long, pale cock, and guided himself inside me with a long, slow glide. He gritted his teeth and said, "This okay?"

"Yes," I answered in breathless abandon.

"Not... hurting... you?" Warren was holding back for my sake.

"Need it." As I threw my arms around his neck, he seated himself fully inside me.

Panting, he let my body adjust. The tightness relented, allowing him to slide deeper, and I savored every pulse of sensation radiating from my core. I could feel the heat of his skin against mine, the rhythm of his heart steadying my own chaos. A soft moan escaped me, and I arched my back, encouraging him to move.

"Good," he breathed, his voice low and gravelly, sending shivers down my spine. "I want to hear that again."

With a gentle thrust, he filled me up, and I gasped, my nails digging into the muscle of his back as pleasure spread like wildfire through my veins.

"Warren..." My voice was a whisper, laced with need. I felt his breath hitch, and it drove me to urge him on.

He began moving slowly, his hips driving in and out with an agonizing precision, each thrust hitting the spot that sent tremors through me. I was lost in the rhythm, the sound of skin against skin echoing in the air, mingling with our heavy breaths.

"Tell me what you want," he whispered against my ear, and it sent another wave of desire crashing over me.

"I want more," I gasped, feeling intoxicated by the moment. "Don't hold back."

With that, his control wavered. He withdrew almost completely before driving back in with a force that left me breathless and craving more. "You asked for it." His voice danced over my skin, rough and demanding.

The intensity built with every thrust, and I felt the world around us blur. The dreamscape faded, only him and pleasure pooling in my core remained. I met his movements with my own, our bodies moving in perfect harmony.

"Like that," I urged, needing to feel him deeper, harder. My body clung to him, desperately seeking the sweet release that loomed above the horizon.

He complied, heightening the pace, each thrust sending sweet shockwaves of pleasure coursing through me.

"You're so beautiful like this," he murmured, his eyes locked onto mine, dark and fierce with desire.

With every thrust, I felt myself spiraling closer to the edge.

"Warren..." My voice trembled, and he sensed the shift in my body, the way I began to clench around him.

"Yes, just like that. Let go for me."

I could feel his own need, for both blood and sexual gratification. Before I could feel even a twinge of fear, he bit the tree above my head and gripped my legs. A third hand, or rather, something fleshy and soft protected my backside as he pounded me. I felt a certain satisfaction being pinned and slammed into.

He reached between us, his fingers finding the sensitive spot that ignited my senses, and I cried out, pleasure crashing over me in a tidal wave. My body shuddered as I surrendered to the bliss, my world collapsing into a bright burst of ecstasy.

As I rode the aftershocks, his thrusts became erratic, his breaths heavy, and I wrapped my legs around him, pulling him deeper, urging him on.

"Come with me," I begged softly. "I want to feel you."

He whimpered, pulling his teeth out of the tree. With a final thrust that pushed us both over the edge, we fused together in that moment of rapture and carried us away on the tide of our tangled desires. We clung to one another, existing only in the aftermath of our shared explosion, pulsating waves of pleasure vibrating through us both.

As the world slowly came back into focus, I smiled at him, breathless and spent. "So, what's next in your domain?"

He smiled, not with teeth, but even this small admission of joy was beautiful. Seeing his lips quirked up made my heart soar.

"Mmmm... I've gotten sidetracked. I will show you what I can do sometime later." He pulled out of me and let my legs down. Our clothes were back on, and I felt squeaky clean as if sex had never happened between us. Back to business then.

Warren stared at me like a messenger with bad news. "Diego's gone missing. Along with your mother. Will you help me find them?"

"Missing?" I found Pepper only to lose her again. "You know, I'm not even surprised."

Thomas absconded with four children. Diego and my mother were missing, presumably together. Warren was a demon on par with one of the most powerful angels known. Then there was little ol' me. Why did I want to get in the middle of this?

Because I wanted to help Warren. I knew what it was like not being able to find an important person. "Alright, but this needs to be on my terms."

"Our terms, Chamomile. We are linked. Your fight is also mine. This connection goes both ways."

"What if I don't want to find her? What if I want to carry on with my life?"

"Then I will do this on my own." He firmed his jaw.

I didn't like that choice either. A cascade of things that could go wrong played with my imagination. What if he bit her and she took control of him? What if he killed her?

"I'll help you, but I..." Our eyes met.

Understanding gleamed in his eyes. "Together," he said. "We'll find them together."

Not the End...

Discover the outcome of Warren and Miles's bond and their search for Diego, Pepper, Thomas, and the children.

Look for Book 2 of Blood Money, the Scarlet Currency series.

DEAR READER

THANK YOU SO MUCH for taking the time to read Blood Money. Carol and I truly appreciate your support and enthusiasm for this story. We're excited to share that we have big plans for this series and will be continuing the journey for quite some time to come.

It's fascinating how the Crimson Currency series came to life. Originally, we envisioned expanding one of our previous stories, The Demon of Reginhart, into a broader series that would explore the lineage of the demon mage, Tiecus, all the way into the present day. The concept of blood dolls captivated us from the very beginning, with our first character, Platt, making her debut in The Demon of Reginhart.

As we delved deeper into this urban paranormal world, we became increasingly enthralled by its possibilities. The thrill of writing this series took hold of us, and before we knew it, we couldn't resist the urge to continue exploring the characters and their intertwined fates. We can't wait to share more about this captivating universe, and hope you'll join us on this thrilling adventure as it unfolds.

Thank you once again for your support, and stay tuned for more!

ABOUT PENN SCRIPTER

Unexpected Paranormal Romance

Penn Scripter is the nom de plume for the writing team of S.N. and Carol McKibben. This mother-daughter combo writes unexpected paranormal romance. Separately, they each have a healthy list of novels.

S.N. McKibben writes dirty stories revolving around social taboos, none of which is for the weak of heart.

Carol McKibben is the author that writes from the eyes of a dog.

The two authors have combined their talents and interests to produce *Unexpected Paranormal Romance* that will include fantasy, mythology, paranormal, dogs and horses, relationships, unusual circumstances, and, of course, romance.

For more information, contact:
stephanie@trollriverpub.com

ALSO BY PENN SCRIPTER

The Demon of Reginhart

MARCUS IS NOT AN ordinary man. He is the only being preventing the demon, Tiecus, and the mage, Asmara, from killing each other and destroying the kingdom. Sent to protect a small port village by King Valder, Marcus finds himself in an unexpected war.

Platt, an unusual local farmgirl, volunteers to help quench the demon's thirst to save her fellow villagers. As strangers living together within his tower, the pending war brings them all closer. Perhaps Platt is what Marcus needs to become whole and no longer in a constant struggle for control.

The fate of them all rests on the outcome of this war, one Marcus is not certain any of them will survive.

AN ODD SENSE of déjà vu enveloped Marcus. He walked, aimless amongst the ancient cedar trees. His nose the only guide until he came to a familiar stream. Across the babbling creek he watched a young girl crouched over a snow berry bush picking at the winter fruit. The scene was as it had been two days ago.

Camouflaged by trees, Marcus watched, fascinated.

A strand of her waist-long hair caught on the bush, and she pushed the cord of white blonde over her shoulder. Delicate fingers claimed berries between leaves and thorns. Crystal blue eyes remained intent on the search for more fruit. She wore the same light blue bodice and cream dress when he'd laid her down and promised vengeance.

This could not be. He'd killed her. He'd felt her die. Yet there she stood, plain as day as if he'd never drained her of life.

Another set of feet puttered down the path on the other side of the river toward the doe. Marcus dipped further behind the large cedar trunk as a youngling approached. The boy was barely beyond his weeling years. He had brown eyes and brown hair and a face pudgy with baby fat. His tunic and pants were the color of a potato sack, but his contrasting cream shirt spilled to his thighs as though the cloth waited for the boy to grow into its size.

"I'm leaving now." The male youngling approached her with a shillelagh in hand. The stick was as straight as one of the arquebus Marcus needed but didn't have the metal casing. "You'll be all right while I'm gone, right?"

"I'm fine, Tim." The doe sighed in exasperation. "Where are you going?"

"Riley called a roust-about." The not-yet youngling puffed his chest out. "Men only."

The doe with clear blue eyes shook her head and smiled. "Men only, huh?"

"I'm old enough!" Tim cried. "Ma said I could go."

The girl—nearly a woman—continued to pluck berries from between dark green leaves. "How manly, asking permission from your mother to go to an all-men's meeting."

"That's right." Tim puffed his scrawny chest out. "Only a fool would defy mom."

The doe scoffed good-naturedly and waved for the youngling to go. "Have fun then."

"I will." Tim strode west carrying a pack, a walking stick, and pride in his step.

After the youngling left, Marcus snuck closer for a more careful assessment of the female. She had no magical residue, so no necromancer raised her from the dead. She had a heartbeat, so she wasn't a golem. And she was much too serene to be riddled by a demon—plus, no shimmer of incandescent light shone from her eyes. She hummed while she scouted for berries, and it was the same tune she'd sung when they first met.

A thin scar stretched under her jugular. It was new and angry.

Shame hit Marcus fast as any punch to the gut. His angst found release in clawing the tree he hid behind. Dust sprinkled the snow, and debris tinkled on the way down.

She turned to the noise, took one look at him, and gave out a mousy squeak. Dropping her possessions, she lurched back. Her basket rustled when it hit compacted snow.

Demon-side instincts surged.

Marcus froze.

In a moment of uncertainty, gauging if she would run or stay, Marcus clamped down on Tiecus's hunger. He'd kill her again if she ran. "Easy..." he held up a hand in warning, urging her to understand and remain steady.

She regained herself, standing still as a lamp post, controlling her breaths. She looked downcast in his direction and remained in place. "Good day, sir." She swallowed and inhaled. "I didn't hear you."

"You are wise, Little Doe." Marcus relaxed and straightened to his full height. "Most humans run, and it is their last mistake."

Her thin frame shook. She wasn't looking into his eyes, preventing Tiecus from playing his game of blink.

She held her fists at her side. Her fear, a pungent musk, filled his nose. "It's said some suffer a worse fate by looking into your eyes."

The little doe was right. He could grabble with her mind and get information from just one look. But that option left him wary. After an experience with a dead human, he never wanted to use his demens, his ability to probe a mind, on anything remotely dead. He still wasn't sure she was fullyalive. If he could help it, the option of talking was best.

Marcus inched forward, careful not to frighten her. "You are Platt?"

Her eyes grew wide in recognition. The scent of fear blasted his nose like a tornado. Her calm demeanor shattered. The little doe turned...

Before she could escape, Marcus leaped.

Platt collided straight into him before she even took twosteps. A soundless cry came from her open mouth, and she began to back away. Her arms up as if she could shield herself from what came next.

Talking wasn't going to be an option. Her eyes met his, and it was all he needed to gain access into her brain. He shoved his will through her eyes, and his consciousness went screaming down a tunnel of blue. "Halt."

A demens created an omniscient effect of two minds blurring. Her mind and his created a mirror effect. He could see through her and through himself. Nausea threatened his equilibrium. Their minds spun, recoiling in the different patterns of thoughts, visions, memories.

He reached for the core inside her brain controlling her motor functions and took hold.

Platt jerked from his possession.

Her fear became his. Torment chased after Marcus. Death. Blackness. Then life. Weakness. Pain. He didn't want to die, again.

It was cruel torment to make her believe she was walking into death, again.

Marcus stiffened and, like a mirror, Platt did the same, stopping her flight.

Mindful of his sharp claws, he stroked her cheek, touching her like the most exquisite flower he'd ever had the honor to caress. Her skin was warm and soft. After years of solitude, such extravagance could become addicting.

His hand slipped to the shiny scar on her throat. "How long does it take a human to heal?"

I don't know, Platt replied from the inside of her thoughts. She'd heard and answered him.

Marcus held her by the shoulders and looked deeper into her eyes. With a mental thrust he pushed his consciousness through the windows of her soul. His thrust was met without resistance, and her core, her very being, her naked, unyielding truth was his to observe.

White hot essence filtered in circles around the calm of her soul. She had three spheres that were in constant motion. They coalesced then separated, always in a methodic slowness but never in the same direction. Her soul was as beautiful as three suns passing through each other. When they joined, the color was translucent. When they separated, one swirled colors like a demon's eyes. Another remained solid yellow, and the last faded between green and blue depending on the others' trajectory.

Her will pushed against his, but she did not have the experience to kick him out. No demon lurked in the recess of her body waiting to possess her. No necromancer controlled her like a puppet. She was the only personality, but there was something else...

Her soul shone flawlessly.

Nothing short of a miracle and timing must have prevailed to save her life.

He no longer pushed for information and did not make her recall the past. What he'd seen of her was more vulnerable than any memory.

He turned his focus to the way back. Thought sparks of red shimmered among an unfamiliar pattern of blue pinpricks like a universe of stars. The colors were merging. Their thoughts were melding together. He sped down a path that suddenly jerked, separating, and then connecting to another road. Marcus didn't have much time before the streets of her thoughts shifted and merged with others. Panic slowly crept into his thoughts. He could get trapped in her mind.

Light washed over him. A belt tightened around his being and tugged.

Snapping back into his own mind was much like allowing Tiecus control of his body. He felt disorientated and took a moment to gather his wits. He was back, alone with his two other companions.

The Reincarnation of Charlie

WHAT IF, AFTER DEATH, we were somehow allowed to take care of those we leave behind?

Some things in life are unexplainable. How it ends is not always what we expect.

Charlie Wolf looked forward to a long life. But what he wanted was not in the cards. Charlie had it all. A loving wife, a booming business, and a horse ranch that made them both happy. Then he was gone.

Heaven can wait.

Soon after his death, Charlie's spirit discovers his wife, Remi, could not recover from losing her soul mate. Remi lost interest in life and even her will to compete in horse shows. The loss of her husband sent Remi into a downward spiral of hopelessness.

Charlie knew that the one thing he had to finish was making sure that his wife Remi could go on. This is their story and how the universe allowed Charlie to end it.

"So, I'm DEAD." Charlie dropped his hands to his sides. That made sense. The accident. The truck crushing him. Waking up in this weird place, naked. "This isn't a dream."

George gave a tight, patient smile. "Does it feel like a dream?"

"I don't feel any different." Hope filtered in his voice.

The spirit guide shook his head. "You know in your heart what's true."

He did. Yet it was still wrong. "It just happened so fast."

"Yes, well, sometimes it's better that way. So, about your other life—"

"Wait!" Charlie took two steps forward. "What about Remi?"

"Remi?" The spirit guide flipped through his chart again, eyes scanning the board. "Or, yes, your wife. I am so sorry about what happens to her . . ."

Charlie jerked up to his full height. "What do you mean? What happens to Remi?"

George slapped his hand over his mouth and back away. "Forget I said that . . . I . . . I wasn't supposed to say anything. But it'll be all right. You won't remember anything in the next life." He looked down at his toes, wiggled them, rolled his eyes, and looked upward at the sound of soft rumbling. "I'm sorry."

Charlie grabbed the little guide by both shoulders this time and shook him. "You'd better tell me right now what's happened to Remi!"

"I . . . I can't . . . I'm not supposed to. I'm new. You're my first case. I made a mistake." The guide, his eyes wide, backed away.

Charlie took in a deep ragged breath. "What happened to Remi? It's only been a few minutes since . . . since my accident."

George sighed. "Well, you see, time doesn't work the same here as it does down there. What's minutes in purgatory is months down there." George cautiously took Charlie by the arm and led him to two clear acrylic-looking chairs. "Here, sit down."

"So, how long has it been?"

George scanned his clipboard. "It's been six months since you passed on in Earth time."

Charlie didn't sit and faced George while trying to absorb what seemed impossible. "Please, for the love of God, if you've ever been alive or ever loved someone, please, please tell me what's happened to Remi."

George grimaced and shook his head. He wasn't going to tell him.

The air constricted around Charlie. If anything happened to his wife because of his carelessness, it wouldn't matter what next life he had; it would be haunted by the memory of losing someone he'd loved with all his being. Of letting the one person that mattered down.

Charlie stared at the board in George's hands and made a split-second decision. He grabbed the clipboard out of the guide's possession, turned, and started flipping through the notes.

"Hey! Give that back!" George leaped out of his chair and grabbed for the board, but Charlie circled and started running while reading.

"You're not going to remember any of this!" George panted, following Charlie. "I'm a spirit guide, not a spirit chaser . . . Oh posh! Come back here."

But what Charlie read stopped him in his tracks.